P9-DEH-277

The Third Tale from
THE FIVE KINGDOMS

THE HEART OF GLASS

VIVIAN FRENCH

ILLUSTRATED BY ROSS COLLINS

CANDLEWICK PRESS

This is a work of fiction. Names, characters, places, and incidents are either products of the author's imagination or, if real, are used fictitiously.

Text copyright © 2010 by Vivian French
Illustrations copyright © 2010 by Ross Collins

All rights reserved. No part of this book may be reproduced, transmitted, or stored in an information retrieval system in any form or by any means, graphic, electronic, or mechanical, including photocopying, taping, and recording, without prior written permission from the publisher.

First U.S. paperback edition 2011

The Library of Congress has cataloged the hardcover edition as follows:

French, Vivian.
The heart of glass : the third tale from the Five Kingdoms /
Vivian French ; illustrated by Ross Collins. — 1st ed.
p.   cm.
Summary: Gracie Gillypot and Prince Marcus embark on
a dwarf-watching outing, not knowing that the dwarves
are working frantically making crowns for a royal wedding
and that they have enlisted some unreliable trolls to help
them, thus putting the humans' expedition in peril.
ISBN 978-0-7636-4814-5 (hardcover)
[1. Fairy tales.] I. Collins, Ross, ill. II. Title
PZ8.F897He 2010
[Fic]—dc22   2009032504

ISBN 978-0-7636-5132-9 (paperback)

11 12 13 14 15 16 BVG 10 9 8 7 6 5 4 3 2 1

Printed in Berryville, VA, U.S.A.

This book was typeset in Baskerville.

Candlewick Press
99 Dover Street
Somerville, Massachusetts, 02144

visit us at www.candlewick.com

For Big Phil, with love, thanks,
and much admiration

PRINCIPAL CHARACTERS

Prince Marcus	second in line to the throne of Gorebreath
Gracie Gillypot	a Trueheart
Marlon	a bat
Alf	Marlon's nephew
Millie	Marlon's daughter
Flo	a bat (No relation to Marlon. Or Alf. Or Millie.)
Gubble	a domesticated troll
Queen Kesta	Queen of Dreghorn
Princess Fedora	Queen Kesta's oldest daughter
Princess Marigold	Queen Kesta's third daughter
Great-Aunt Hortense	Dowager Duchess of Cockenzie Rood
Queen Bluebell	Queen of Wadingburn
Prince Vincent	Queen Bluebell's grandson
Professor Scallio	Prince Vincent's tutor
Fingle	Queen Bluebell's coachman
King Thab	King of the Underground Trolls
Spittle	King Thab's scribe
Mullius Gowk	an Old Troll, servant to King Thab
Clod	an Underground Troll
Oolie	half Old Troll, half goblin, wholly evil
Bestius Bonnyrigg	a dwarf
Master Amplethumb	a dwarf

THE ANCIENT CRONES

Edna	the Ancient One
Elsie	the Oldest
Val	the Youngest
Foyce	Gracie's stepsister and apprentice crone

Chapter One

"If I were you, kiddo," the bat remarked, "I'd close your mouth. Dangerous, leaving it open like that. Never know what might pop in. Flies, midges, the odd moth. Furry things, moths. Not nice unless you're used to them."

Prince Marcus, second in line to the throne of Gorebreath, did as he was told. "But where IS she?" His voice was shaking. "One minute she was leaning against that tree, and then — *WHOOOMPH!* She was gone!" He rubbed his eyes. "And was it that tree? Or that one? They all look exactly the same! Did you see, Marlon?"

"Cool it, kid," the bat said. "Alf's ahead of you. Alf? Where are you?"

"Here, Unc!" The small squeak came from some ways away.

Marcus stared at Marlon. "What's he doing?"

"Hanging on a branch." Marlon sounded pleased. "Marking the tree. Good work, Alf!"

Marcus shook his head. "That can't be right. Gracie was here beside me. I *know* she was!"

Marlon sighed. "Look at your map, kiddo. Where are we? The Unreliable Forest. Now the thing about unreliable forests, in case you hadn't guessed, is that they're unreliable. See a handful of berries you fancy? Walk toward them, and—*FFFFT!* They'll be behind you."

Seeing his companion's doubtful expression, the bat sighed again. "Try it for yourself. Got a hankie? Well, tie it to a branch."

Unwillingly, Marcus did as he was told. The scarlet handkerchief, emblazoned with the royal arms of the House of Gorebreath, fluttered in front of him . . . and vanished.

"That's gone too!" The prince took a step backward and looked at Marlon. "What's going on?"

"Turn around."

Turning, Marcus was just in time to see the tree his hankie was tied to make a sudden sideways leap and hide behind a substantial oak. The oak showed no inclination to move, and Marcus leaned against it, feeling breathless. "That's SO weird," he said. "And however are we going to find Gracie?"

Marlon twitched his wings. "Kiddo," he said, and he sounded far more solemn than usual, "we need help on this one. You stay here. Keep an eye on Alf."

"What?" Marcus stared at the bat. "Where are you going?"

"Trust me, kid. I'll be back pronto." Marlon was circling high in the air. A moment later he was gone.

Chapter Two

It had all started out rather well. Marcus, together with his very good friend Gracie Gillypot, had been planning a dwarf-spotting expedition for some time. It was well known that the dwarves had an access tunnel in the middle of the Unreliable Forest of Flailing. Marlon had told Gracie that Monday was the best day to visit, as that was when the dwarves emerged to deal with Aboveground Business, and she and Marcus had made their arrangements accordingly.

A certain amount of subterfuge had been necessary on Marcus's part; not only was Flailing a good half-day's ride beyond the border of the Five Kingdoms (and therefore regarded by his parents with much suspicion), but his home life was far from simple. A good deal of his time was being taken up with rehearsals for a wedding, soon to take place in the Kingdom of

Dreghorn, and he had had to make sure his absence would not cause his mother to collapse in a fit of the vapors. He and his twin brother, Prince Arioso, had been asked to take part in the wedding procession; Arioso, always the perfect prince, was delighted, but Marcus was horrified. At first he had refused to have anything to do with it, but his father, King Frank, issued an ultimatum. "No son of mine," he declared, "will disgrace the Royal House of Gorebreath. If you don't do your duty, young man, you'll not be allowed to leave the palace grounds for the rest of the year. And don't think I don't mean it, because I do!"

Huffing and puffing, Marcus had fought his way to a compromise: He would attend rehearsals and walk in the procession, but he was to be allowed weekends off, together with every other Monday — and no one was to question what he got up to. Or where.

Gracie was more fortunate. After an unpleasant and unhappy early life with a wicked stepfather, during which she was forced to endure the company of a step-sister who was an all-time expert in pure evil, she had managed to escape to the House of the Ancient Crones hidden deep in the hollows of the More Enchanted Hills. The three old women who lived there had adopted her, and she was now free to plan expeditions and outings whenever she felt like it . . . a freedom much envied by Marcus.

"You don't know how lucky you are," he said gloomily as he and Gracie walked out of the House and into the early morning sunlight. "All I get all day and every day are orders and instructions. And I'm supposed to be prancing along in this stupid wedding procession arm in arm with Marigold, and she's the silliest girl I ever met in my entire life."

Gracie, who knew exactly how lucky she was, made soothing noises and tried not to feel pleased that Marcus was so dismissive of Princess Marigold. It wasn't that she was jealous — after all, who could be jealous of someone who was kept awake all night by the thought of a new bottle of nail polish? — but she was very aware that Marigold was positioned right under Marcus's nose by his anxious parents as often as possible. She had also noticed Marigold's tendency to blush and flutter her eyelashes whenever Marcus was nearby.

"It'll all be over soon," she said. "And you never know. Prince Vincent might sweep her off her feet at the reception."

Marcus brightened. "That's not a bad idea," he said. "Maybe I could bribe him. He'll do anything for a box of chocolates."

Gracie smiled and opened the gate. The path showed signs of wanting to follow her, and she frowned at it. "STAY!" she commanded, and waited until it had tucked itself away. "*Good* path," she said, and gave it a farewell wave.

Marcus looked around in surprise. "Isn't Gubble coming with us?"

Gracie shook her head. "He's still asleep in his cupboard. When he wakes up, he's going to make a cake with Auntie Elsie. Chocolate with nuts. With any luck it'll be ready when we get back."

"Are trolls any good at cooking?" Marcus sounded doubtful, and Gracie laughed.

"Auntie Elsie'll make sure it's delicious. Come on— let's get going!" And the two of them set out along the rough track that led away from the House of the Ancient Crones and toward the Unreliable Forest.

To begin with, they walked beside Marcus's pony, Glee, but as the track gradually narrowed, they took turns riding. The trees became more and more twisted and bent on either side, and the undergrowth thicker. Glee shied as a large root snaked suddenly across the path in front of him. Marcus soothed him and stroked his neck, and the pony trotted unwillingly on, his ears flicking to and fro.

"I think we must be nearly there," Gracie said at last. "Listen! Can you hear voices? I can!"

Marcus pulled Glee to a halt. "No . . . I don't think so . . ."

"They're arguing," Gracie reported. "One of them's telling the other—OH!" A huge smile spread across her face. "It's not the dwarves! It's Marlon! And Alf!"

Even as she spoke, the two bats came swinging out from the trees and circled around Glee's head. "Miss Gracie! Miss Gracie!" The smaller bat dived into a loop and came up looking anxious. "Uncle Marlon says you won't want me coming with you to watch the dwarves because it's a . . . a . . . a himposition—but you don't mind, do you?"

"Just tell him to buzz off, kiddo." Marlon was gruff. "Getting above himself. Doesn't know when he's not wanted."

Gracie smiled. "He's very welcome," she said. "It'll be much more fun if the two of you come with us."

"There!" Alf made a face at his uncle, then zoomed out of the reach of his leathery wing. "I told you, Unc, but you wouldn't listen!"

Marlon sighed and settled himself on Marcus's shoulder. "If you're sure. Don't want to spoil any two-by-two stuff."

Marcus winked at Gracie and was surprised to see her blush. She covered it quickly by laughing and shaking her head at Alf. "You'd better be polite to your uncle. I wouldn't be here if it weren't for him. I'd still be living in a pitch-black cellar surrounded by spiders. He's a hero!"

The older bat looked pleased. "All in the line of duty, kid. Now, let's go. Best to leave the pony here, I'd say."

Marcus nodded. He knotted Glee's reins and led him toward a patch of grass. "Wait here, boy," he instructed, and the pony looked around warily before lowering his head to graze.

"Will the dwarves be very hairy?" Alf twittered as Marlon flew ahead. "Will they have beards to their knees?" The older bat heard him and looped back.

"Watch it, Alf. Those guys are ancient. Respect 'n' stuff."

Alf looked suitably apologetic. "Sorry, Uncle Marlon."

As Marlon swooped off to lead the way, Gracie tried to remember what she knew about dwarves. Auntie Val had looked doubtful when she mentioned the expedition, but the Ancient One had pooh-poohed any suggestion that it might be dangerous.

"Our Gracie's a Trueheart," she'd said. "She'll be fine. Dwarves know more about Good and Evil than almost anyone; they've been around such a long time. Can be tricksy, of course, but they're hardworking. Very hardworking. Not like some I could mention . . ." And the Ancient One had given Auntie Val a meaningful stare that had sent her scuttling back to her weaving.

"Dwarves mine for gold, you know," Marcus said, as if he were reading Gracie's thoughts. "Father told me they've got a huge order in for the wedding. Crowns galore." He snorted derisively. "Apparently Queen Kesta is expected to give Fedora and all her sisters new crowns, and Fedora has to have a special one to give Tertius, and then he has to bow and present her with yet another one — and goodness only knows what happens after that. They probably play hoop-la with them all afternoon."

Gracie laughed, then stopped as the narrow pathway made a sudden sharp turn around a bent and twisted tree. In front of her was a green grassy hollow. A tingle ran up and down her spine when she saw that in the center was a large hole and a heap of freshly dug earth.

"Dwarves!" Alf squeaked, and zoomed over Gracie's head.

Gracie jumped and put out her hand to steady herself when dry twiggy fingers wrapped themselves around her wrist. She had no time to cry out; she hardly saw the tree trunk opening before she was hauled deep inside and swallowed up.

Marcus, turning to ask her what they should do next, saw no sign of her. Gracie had vanished.

Chapter Three

Great-Aunt Hortense, otherwise known as Dowager Duchess of the kingdom of Cockenzie Rood, was not happy. "This," she told herself, "is not what I expected." She fished in her ample handbag, pulled out her niece's letter, and began to read aloud. "'*Do* come and stay in Dreghorn for darling Fedora's wedding to precious Prince Tertius, Auntie dear. It'll be *such* fun having you here, and we'll make sure you have a lovely rest. Loads of love and kisses, Kesta.' HMPH! I'd have had more of a rest if I'd stayed at home organizing tea parties for the entire population." She did her best to suppress a sigh and turned her attention back to the third of Queen Kesta's many daughters.

Princess Marigold was standing in front of a heap of discarded dresses, frowning fiercely. "I've nothing to wear," she said accusingly. "Nothing at all. How can I

make Marcus think I'm the wonderfullest and prettiest princess in the whole wide world if I don't have anything to wear?"

"Most wonderful," her great-aunt corrected her. "There's no such word as *wonderfullest*."

Marigold took no notice. "It's SO not fair," she went on. "Fedora's got *everything* new, and Mother won't even buy me a new dress. If I had a sky-blue satin dress covered in tiny pink rosebuds with a hooped petticoat and lace borders, I just *know* Marcus would fall madly in love with me forever and ever. Fedora doesn't need a dress like that—I do!"

The dowager duchess rolled her eyes. Marigold had talked of nothing but new dresses and Marcus for the last three days. Today the somewhat one-sided conversation had started before Hortense had even had her breakfast, and as a result she was both hungry and tetchy. Marcus had been pointed out at the last wedding rehearsal, and Hortense had noticed his unbrushed hair and mud-covered boots, together with his tendency to stand on one leg and gaze out the window when he was meant to be paying attention. He seemed an unlikely candidate for Marigold's affections, even though there was no doubt that he was good-looking. His twin brother, Arioso, neat and tidy and attentive in every way, looked far more suitable, but when Hortense suggested this, Marigold rolled her eyes.

"Arry? Oh, he's madly in love with Nina-Rose. Besides, he's boring. Marcus likes going on adventures and having fun." Marigold put her head on one side and looked wistful. "I wish *I* could go on adventures. He'd be sure to notice me then, but he likes that horrible Gracie Gillypot, and she's not even a princess! She's just *ordinary*. AND she's got a friend who's a troll!"

Marigold's great-aunt studied her thoughtfully. She was well aware that Marigold, in common with her many sisters, was not a clever girl. Pretty, opinionated, and somewhat spoiled, but not clever. Her eldest sister was about to be married to Prince Tertius of Niven's Knowe, and no doubt the two of them would live together comfortably enough to rate as a "happy ever after." Nina-Rose apparently had her eye on Arioso; they too would make a delightfully dull royal couple. Was Marigold any different? Possibly. It was certainly unusual for any princess from the Five Kingdoms to express an interest in adventure.

The old duchess stroked her chin. She had had many adventures in her youth and firmly believed that they had made her a more interesting person. Perhaps some kind of carefully contrived expedition into the world beyond the kingdoms would knock some of the foolishness out of Marigold's brain. Hortense nodded. It was worth a try. After all, anything was better than hearing Marigold endlessly complain about the contents of her wardrobe.

"What kind of adventures does Prince Marcus like, exactly?" she asked.

Marigold's eyes began to shine. "He helped rescue Fedora and Nina-Rose from a horrible sorceress! And he found Queen Bluebell's long-lost granddaughter as well. He's . . . he's WONDERFUL. And I heard him telling Arry that he was going on a hunt to find the dear little dwarves who make our crowns for us, and he wanted nasty Gracie to go with him." Marigold pouted. "What's so special about *her*?"

Her great-aunt thought of pointing out that anyone who had been invited to live with the powerful Ancient Crones must be very special indeed, but decided this was not the right moment. Instead she said, "Have you thought of going to see the dwarves for yourself?"

Marigold's mouth fell open.

"Tut, child!" Hortense frowned. "That is a most unattractive look. I repeat, have you thought of going to see the dwarves for yourself? Flailing is the place, I believe. The Unreliable Forest."

Marigold gulped. "But . . . but that's miles and miles outside the border! We're not allowed. There are horrible things out there. Really, really, REALLY horrible!"

"I thought you wanted to have an adventure!" Hortense's tone sharpened.

"I do!" Marigold wailed. "But I want a nice *safe* adventure here in the Five Kingdoms!"

There was a moment's silence while the duchess gathered her thoughts. "Perhaps you could go just a little way beyond the border — a place where Prince Marcus would come across you on his return? That would be quite safe, but it would show a splendid spirit."

"But I can't!" Marigold looked horrified. "What if I meet" — her not very active imagination did its best — "a wasp?"

"Then, Marigold," her great-aunt snapped, "you will run away screaming. And with any luck your gallant prince will come galloping up to rescue you. He does have a horse, I presume?"

Marigold nodded enthusiastically. "Oh, yes! It's the sweetest little pony called Glee! And he just adores carrots! He's got dear little whiskers on his nose, and—"

"Thank you, dear. That's quite enough information." Hortense raised a warning finger. "And it might be wise to curb your enthusiasm just a smidgen."

Marigold looked blank. "Pardon?"

"Less of the 'sweet little this' and 'dear little that,'" her great-aunt explained. "Boys don't care for it."

"Oh." Marigold thought about this, frowning deeply. At last her face cleared. "You mean I shouldn't talk about the pony?"

Hortense gave up. "Don't worry about it, dear. It was foolish of me to mention it." She heaved herself to her feet and headed for the door. "Excuse me, but I need my breakfast. I need it badly. I'll see you later."

Marigold watched her great-aunt go. *What's the matter with her?* she wondered. *Old people are so strange. And fancy suggesting I go to see the dwarves!* She shook her head. *How would I ever find the way? Although . . .* Her thoughts went back to Hortense's other suggestion. *Although perhaps I could go to the border and wait for Marcus to come back.* Marigold began to suck her finger, a sure sign that she was planning something of advantage to herself. *If I borrowed Fedora's dear little pony and cart, it wouldn't take me very long. Her pony goes ever so quickly. I won't bother to ask her because she's busy having her singing lesson, and I'm sure Mother would tell me not to interrupt. Besides, Fedora might say no. She's SO selfish.* A self-pitying sigh. *Much better not to say anything. And once I reach the edge of the Five Kingdoms, I can sit under the trees by the edge of the path and pick some flowers and make a wreath for my hair. That'll look ever so pretty. I bet horrid Gracie Gillypot wouldn't think of something as clever as that.* Marigold smiled smugly. *And when Prince Marcus comes riding by he'll see me, and he'll think, "There's Princess Marigold, and she's having an adventure too!" He'll be SO surprised. And then I'll scream, and he'll save me, and I'll ride back home with him . . .* The smile spread. *And we'll live happily ever after!*

Chapter Four

Mullius Gowk was in a bad mood. If he'd had more than one tooth to grind, he would have ground them. His master, King Thab, lord of all trolls, was quite unaware of his glowering and muttering. This was not surprising, as Mullius in a bad mood was not very different from Mullius in his normal state of mind. He always stamped, he always growled, and he always took every possible opportunity to block the path of anyone wishing to get past his substantial bulk. If he could cause grievous bodily harm by crushing the passerby against a jagged rock or two, then so much the better. Mullius was an Old Troll, and he remembered the days when even the most wicked of witches trembled when a troll came by. Old Trolls had status then. And power. The High King of the Old Trolls had never known the meaning of the word *mercy*. He had lived for hundreds of years and had never once done a good deed. Some said his heart was made of stone, others that it was lead. After his death there had been stories told at many a troll fireside, stories of his unrelenting cruelty and unceasing quest for domination.

Mullius flexed his enormous muscles, and his muttering turned to a low-level snarl. He was the last of the Old Trolls; the new trolls (a mere two or three hundred years old) were a very different lot. They had gone against all Old Troll traditions and signed contracts and treaties with the rulers of the Five Kingdoms, and now there were laws about Keeping to Your Designated Caverns. There were even notices pinned up in King Thab's apartments that suggested "A smile a day keeps the blues away." Mullius had never smiled. Not even when he was a young troll, allowed to bludgeon dwarves and goblins and gnomes into a pulp whenever he felt like it. Those had been fine times, but they were long gone, along with the High King.

Mullius alone was left. It was his size and strength that had saved him; King Thab, despite having signed a contract promising to banish all Old Trolls to the depths of the Invincible Caverns, was vain enough to think that a towering mass of matted black hair and muscle would impress visitors. Mullius was his official guard and also the keeper of the iron box — King Thab's most precious possession. Only Mullius and the king knew what the box contained; when King Thab's wife, Queen Thulka, had tried to bribe Mullius into lifting the lid, he, with the king's reluctant agreement, had carried her back to her mother while she wept all the way. The king had been glumly grateful ever since; Mullius remained impassive, and the iron box never left his side. If he had any hopes — other than the opportunity to indulge in some serious bludgeoning resulting in a great deal of bloody carnage — he kept them to himself. In the meantime he was forced to watch King Thab and his companions being polite — insofar as a troll was ever polite — to creatures that Mullius regarded as little more than pie filling.

Mullius's scowl grew deeper. "Grind. Crush. Slay," he muttered. "Blood. Guts. Kill." He gave King Thab an evil glare. "Dwarves! No dwarves. Dwarves in dwarf place. Not here!"

King Thab remained oblivious. He was sitting on his rocky throne in the semidarkness of the royal apartments, and he was thinking. On a stone slab in front of him was a sheet of yellow parchment covered in dwarvish writing, and beside him a small goblin

clutching a large pencil was poised over a slate. Behind the stone slab stood a stocky white-bearded dwarf, who was doing his best to ignore Mullius and his mutterings. "We wouldn't normally bother you, sir," the dwarf said, "and I'm sorry to call on you so early in the day. But things are getting a bit out of hand. We've been digging nonstop for three weeks now, and — like it says in the letter — Master Amplethumb doesn't think we're going to be on time. We hoped —" He coughed and gave King Thab an encouraging smile. "We hoped we might be able to interest you in some sort of exchange."

"Eh?" King Thab looked blank.

"Some sort of exchange," the dwarf repeated. "You know . . . You help us out by sending a troll or two to do a bit of digging, and we'll help you in return."

"Return?" The king's expression of total incomprehension remained unchanged.

"Payment, sir." The dwarf was doing his best to stay calm. Master Amplethumb had told him that King Thab was sometimes a little slow to understand letters and messages. "Be patient, Bestius," he had warned. "Remember, he's a troll. Their brains are, shall we say, differently wired?"

Bestius took a deep breath and went back to his

explanation. "Like I said. A payment. A reward for helping us. We'd like to give you something in return for your help."

"I get troll back. Dwarves return troll." The king looked pleased with himself.

"Well. Yes, we'll certainly undertake to do that." The dwarf decided to try a different approach and dug in his pockets. "Here," he said, and held out a chain made of the finest gold. "Master Amplethumb asked me to give you this as an example of what we could offer you. Perhaps your lady would like it?"

There was a warning rumble from Mullius, and the goblin's pencil snapped between his fingers. King Thab sprang from his seat with a furious snarl . . . but as Bestius took an alarmed step backward, the king sank down again, groaned, and put his heavy head on the stone slab. The goblin caught the dwarf's eye and mouthed, "Best not to mention ladies. Sore point. Could cause trouble." He hesitated, then added, "I could look after it for you, if you like."

Bestius hastily slid the necklace back into his pocket. "Sorry if I've caused any offense," he said. "Maybe we could offer something else instead?"

There was no response from the troll king.

"Time to go," the goblin whispered. "Not the right

moment just now. Come again later." He crept closer. "You could bring more gold . . ."

The dwarf bowed politely but did not move. His orders had been clear. "Erm . . . very sorry and all that, but I have to report back to Master Amplethumb. It's a matter of some urgency, you see. We must have help. Don't want to let the Royal Family down. There's kings and queens and princes and rows and rows of pretty princesses all waiting for brand-new crowns, and if we don't deliver on time — why, we dwarves'll never be asked to work again."

For a moment there was complete silence. Then King Thab slowly lifted his head. "Pretty princesses?"

"That's right." The dwarf nodded. "It's an order for a wedding, see? Prince Tertius and Princess Fedora are getting hitched. Loads of pretty princesses, and princes and —"

"STOP!" King Thab's huge fist crashed down on the letter in front of him — but there was something like a smile on his toothless face. He turned to the goblin. "Write, Spittle," he ordered. "Write, 'Agree. Trolls will dig. Agree.'"

Spittle's mouth opened wide in astonishment, and Mullius growled.

"Silence!" King Thab waved an imperious arm. "Write, Spittle."

"Yes, Your Majesty. Of course, Your Majesty." The goblin's pencil squeaked furiously on the slate. "Erm . . . how about, 'Thab, King of All Trolls, presents his compliments to Master Amplethumb, and is delighted and ekstatik' "— Spittle paused and crossed the last word out—" 'Is delighted and happy to agree to his request for assistance in the matter of extracting gold from the valleys of Flailing. Thab, King of All Trolls, is willing to offer . . .' " Spittle paused again and put down his pencil. "Excuse me, Your Majesty, but how many trolls will you be sending?"

Thab turned to the dwarf. "How many? He ask."

"One or two would be sufficient, sir," the dwarf told him, "trolls being that much bigger than us dwarves. And stronger," he added with a sideways glance at Mullius.

"That's right. That was in Master Amplethumb's letter, Your Majesty." The goblin picked up the parchment. "Erm . . . here we are. 'The pressures upon us are immense owing to the forthcoming wedding in the Kingdom of Dreghorn. All our able-bodied dwarves are already actively employed in the extraction of gold, but I fear the order will not be ready in time unless you are able to assist us. One, or at most two, of your strongest trolls would be invaluable.'"

The king nodded. "Yes. Write, 'Agree. One troll. One troll to dig.'"

Spittle's pencil began to squeak again. "'. . . is willing to offer one troll, with his warmest wishes for your success in this venture.'"

He put down his pencil, but the king snatched it up and thrust it back into his hand. "Write more, Spittle. Exchange! Payment! Write, 'Troll dig for dwarves. Exchange pretty princess.' Pretty for me—for King Thab!" Exhausted by this effort, the king lay back in his throne and closed his eyes, thus missing the expression of total horror on the dwarf's face.

Spittle gave a sly chuckle and went on: "'In exchange for this act of generosity, King Thab will expect delivery of a princess—'"

"Pretty!" interrupted the king without opening his eyes.

"So sorry, Your Majesty. I was about to add that requirement. 'One PRETTY princess, to keep His Most Royal Majesty company.'"

Bestius stood first on one foot, then on the other, as Spittle went on writing. He was one of the older dwarves and a leading member of the Underworld

Council, but he was, for once, at a loss. How could he promise a princess in return for a troll? The dwarves had as little contact as possible with the aboveground inhabitants of the Five Kingdoms; long experience had taught them that humans became unreliable, if not downright untrustworthy, when large quantities of gold were involved. "Your Majesty," he began, "there . . . there might be a bit of a problem."

The king of the trolls frowned. "No problem. No. No pretty, no troll."

"Ah." Bestius pulled at his beard. Judging by King Thab's expression, the matter was best left alone for the moment. He made a decision. Master Amplethumb had asked for a troll; Master Amplethumb could solve any ensuing difficulties. Bowing, he said, "Agreed."

The king grunted. Mullius rumbled. Spittle finished writing with a flourish and handed the slate to his master. "If you could just sign here, Your Majesty, our friend can take it to Master Amplethumb. I presume you'll be sending the troll today? It's early enough for him to do a full day's work, and I've indicated as much in the letter."

King Thab laboriously inscribed a cross at the bottom of the slate, then turned back to the goblin. "Clod," he ordered. "Fetch Clod."

"Certainly, Your Majesty," said Spittle. Springing to his feet, he handed the slate to the dwarf. "Here. You'd better wait." And then he was gone.

Bestius waited, very aware of Mullius's looming and unfriendly bulk. King Thab took no notice of either of them; he was gazing into space, a faint smile on his face.

Time ticked on, until at last there was the sound of heavy footsteps echoing from the other side of the cavernous apartment. Bestius glanced up and blinked. Clod, following obediently behind the goblin, was easily as large as Mullius but had four arms. In each hand, he clutched a heavy iron spade, and he was encrusted with mud.

Spittle tittered as he saw the expression of astonishment on the dwarf's face. "He's a digging machine," he explained. "Solve all your problems in a couple of hours, I'd say. Good luck, and don't forget to bring him back when you've finished with him." He gave Bestius a sideways look. "And remember to bring the pretty princess back with you. Not a good idea to mess with trolls, you know. But you'd better get going!" He slapped the monster's leg and pointed at Bestius. "Follow him, Clod. Follow . . . and do as you're told."

"Yug," Clod said.

"Oh. Well. Thank you very much." Bestius was still in a state of shock. "It—I mean, he—will be perfect. We'll see you again soon. Very soon." He bowed, then turned and marched out of the room toward the wide, stone-floored tunnel that led away from the royal palace, Clod stomping meekly after him.

Chapter Five

Gubble was carefully measuring out the ingredients for the chocolate cake when Marlon came flitting through the open window.

Elsie, otherwise known as the Oldest Crone, looked up in surprise. "I thought you were showing Gracie and Marcus the way to the Unreliable Forest," she said.

Marlon swung himself onto the curtain rail and hung upside down while he got his breath back. "Bit of a snag," he reported.

"Really?" Elsie's eyebrows rose. "Nothing serious, I hope?"

"Nope. Maybe. Yes." Marlon shuffled along the rail. "It's Gracie."

Gubble gave an anxious grunt, and Elsie went pale. "Gracie? What's happened? Surely the dwarves wouldn't hurt a Trueheart!"

"Not the dwarves," Marlon told her. "A tree. Gracie leaned against it." He waved a wing. "Next minute — gone!"

"Oh, dear." Elsie put her hand to her face. "I think we'd better tell the Ancient One."

Gubble frowned. "Find Gracie," he said. "NOW." And he headed toward the back door, which immediately slipped to one side and pretended to be a window.

The Oldest rushed after him and towed him back. "Let's hear what Edna has to say first, shall we?" she suggested, and led the way into the corridor. Room seventeen, the most important room in the House of the Ancient Crones, was, for once, immediately opposite, and Elsie sighed with relief as she and Gubble hurried in.

The two looms were click-click-clacking as usual; an extremely pretty young woman was angrily throwing the shuttle to and fro on the smaller loom, while the Ancient One was steadily weaving the iridescent silver of the web of power. Val, the Youngest Crone, was muttering to herself as she tried to sort out a tangle of thread on the floor.

"Edna," said Elsie, "could you spare a minute? Marlon's just arrived with some rather alarming news."

The Ancient One glanced around, her one blue eye gleaming. "Can't be too alarming. The web's clear. Look!"

All three crones stared at the loom, and indeed the gleaming silver cloth flowed smooth and stain-free.

The pretty girl sneered. "What's the matter? Has my nasty little stepsister gotten herself lost? Serves her right. Perhaps she's been eaten by a bear. Crunch, crunch — Gracie for lunch!"

"Be silent, Foyce," Edna said. "Remarks like that will most certainly prolong your stay here. We can release only those who are purged of wickedness and evil." Her voice was quiet, but the girl flinched and bent low over her work. The Ancient One turned to Val. "Val, dear, could you take over for five minutes? I'll have a word with Marlon, and then I'll be straight back."

The Youngest nodded and took Edna's place in front of the web. As she did so, a faint shadow rippled across the shimmering sheet of silver, and both old women caught their breath, but a second later it was gone.

"Hmm." The Ancient One sounded thoughtful. "Keep a close eye on it, dear. It looks as if something might be stirring after all. I'll go and see what Marlon has to say."

* * *

Marlon was fretting. Only his deep respect and admiration for the Ancient Crones stopped him from flying into room seventeen and asking them to hurry things along. When Gubble came stomping back into the kitchen, Marlon flew down to perch on a chair back and asked, "Well? Action stations or what?"

"Unk," Gubble said as he marched across the room, a determined expression on his flat green face. "Get Gracie. Gubble go."

"Yay!" Marlon said approvingly. "What did the crones say?"

Gubble ignored him. Reaching the back door — which was where it belonged but upside down — he grunted loudly. The door shot up to the ceiling, and Gubble folded his arms and grunted again. When there was no response, he walked through the wall, leaving a troll-shaped space behind him, together with a great deal of fresh air.

Marlon began to laugh but stopped as Edna and Elsie came in from the corridor. He waved a wing at the gaping hole. "Gubble's gone."

"We can see that for ourselves," the Ancient One said crisply. "Now, please tell us exactly what happened."

Marlon stood at attention and gave a short but accurate account of the early morning's events.

When he had finished, Edna nodded. "Very sensible to mark the tree. Well done." Marlon glowed — but he looked increasingly uneasy as she went on. "It sounds like a dwarf-trap, but I can't be sure. I thought they'd all been sealed up long ago, but it's possible one or two of them were forgotten about. Nasty things, dwarf-traps."

Elsie frowned. "What were the dwarves hoping to catch?"

"Oh, it wasn't the dwarves who set them." Edna sounded surprised by Elsie's ignorance. "They'd never do anything like that. It was the trolls. They used to catch dwarves, because . . ." She hesitated, then went on. "Because in those days the trolls liked nothing more than a dwarf for dinner." She saw the Oldest's horrified expression and added, "I'm talking about a *very* long time ago, Elsie dear."

Marlon leaned forward. "So — we're talking traps. One way only? In but no out?"

"I would imagine so." Edna pondered for a moment. "I suggest Marcus try to talk to the dwarves. I'm sure they could dig Gracie out again. . . . I imagine she's fallen into some kind of pit."

"Marcus — dwarves — chitchat — rescue — happy ever after. Check." Marlon stretched his wings. "Better be off."

Edna held up her hand. "One moment. The dwarves don't always take kindly to humans, especially if the humans are asking for a favor."

"But Marcus is a *prince*," Elsie said in shocked tones.

"In my opinion, that's a distinct disadvantage," Edna told her. "It's the Royals who keep the dwarves so hard at work. They're always wanting gold for weddings and suchlike." She fished in her pocket and produced a handful of silver threads. "Here — take these. They're offcuts from the web of power, and they can be quite useful, although you never can tell exactly how they'll work. Pure and unadulterated goodness is an odd commodity. Give a couple of them to the dwarves with my best wishes, and keep a couple for emergencies. Do be careful, though. They can have unexpected side effects."

Marlon looped the threads around his neck, staggered, and fell off the chair. "Got a problem," he announced from the floor.

Elsie hurried forward and removed all but one of the silvery wisps. She looked reproachfully at the Ancient One. "You never remember how heavy these are, Edna. They come from the web, remember. Only Truehearts like you and Gracie think they weigh nothing at all."

"I'm so sorry," Edna said. "Are you all right, Marlon?"

The bat nodded and fluttered back to the chair. Even the single thread seemed to be weighing heavily on his small, furry shoulders, but he held his head up high. "Report soon as mission accomplished," he promised. "Erm . . . what about Gubble?"

The Ancient One smiled. "Let's hope you and Marcus will have rescued Gracie by the time he reaches the Unreliable Forest. He's not the speediest of travelers."

Marlon nodded, wobbled, regained his balance with an effort, and launched himself into the air. "See ya!" he called, and swooped out the window.

Elsie watched him go, then turned to Edna. "Tell me," she said, "I didn't want to ask in front of Marlon—I didn't want to worry him . . . but what if Gracie's fallen into a tunnel? Where would it lead?"

"To the trolls' caverns, most likely." Edna shook her head. "Not a happy thought. The underground trolls are better than they used to be, but they really are a completely different breed from overground trolls like Gubble. Still, at least they sent all the Old Trolls away. They were even nastier than the ogres, and that's saying something."

Elsie looked uneasy. "Wasn't there some rumor that King Thab kept one of the Old Trolls as a bodyguard?"

"What?" The Ancient One's voice was sharp. "Where did you hear that?"

Elsie took her wig off, scratched her head, and replaced the wild red curls. "I really can't remember. I could be wrong, of course."

"Let's hope you are," Edna said. "You should have told me about that as soon as you heard it. And while you're busy digging around in your memories of the past, is there anything else I should know?"

"Well . . ." Elsie hesitated. "I was wondering, how do underground trolls feel about Truehearts? Isn't there an old story about a Trueheart and a troll king?"

The Ancient One sat down hard on a kitchen chair. "Oh, my goodness. You're right. The prophecy . . . Oh, Elsie, how could I have forgotten?" She frowned for a moment, then sighed. "It's no use worrying about it. We must hope the dwarves find our Gracie safe and sound . . . and then, as soon as she's back here, we can warn her. No more exploring—or, at least, not where there might be underground trolls."

"Or Old Trolls," Elsie added.

Edna nodded, pulled herself to her feet, and set off for the door. "I think we'd better check the web right this minute."

Elsie hurried after her.

They heard Val calling them before they even got through the door of room seventeen — and by the time they reached the loom, it was all too clear that ugly mud-colored stains were creeping across the sheet of silver. "What does it mean?" Val asked anxiously. "Doesn't that color mean trolls?"

Gracie's stepsister, busy untangling knots on the other loom, snorted. "I can tell you what it means," she said. "It means trouble. Trouble for your darling Gracie — and it serves the little worm right!"

Chapter Six

High in the air, Marlon came swooping over the forest. Looking down, he saw Marcus sitting on the grass, his back against the comforting solidity of an oak tree; clearly there had been no dramatic developments. As Marlon swung into a dive, however, the silver thread slipped off his shoulders and fell into a particularly thick tangle of gorse below; he muttered and flew after it, but the sun was in his eyes and he could not see where it had fallen. He circled the gorse bushes several times, trying to find a perch among the prickles, but there was no glint of silver anywhere.

Marlon gulped and headed for the top of the oak tree to do some serious thinking. He had acted as the crones' messenger for many years, and he had never lost a message or a token before. He debated making a return visit to confess, but on consideration decided against it. "Marlon Batster, me," he told himself aloud. "Bat of action. Hero to Gracie Gillypot. I can sort it out. No prob." And ignoring any lingering doubts, he flew a victory roll before spiraling to join Marcus.

Marcus had long since given up hoping that Marlon would come back with the news that it was all a mistake and Gracie was happily at home with the Ancient Crones, and he was trying his hardest not to feel too gloomy. Yawning, he looked around to see where Alf had gone. "Alf!" he called. "Alf? Where are you?"

There was a twittering in the distance. "Here, Mr. Prince. I'm marking the tree, but it keeps moving . . ."

Hearing the underlying note of panic in Alf's voice, Marcus got to his feet and went to find him. The small bat was clinging to the branches of a silver birch—but as Marcus strolled toward the tree, it shook itself, side-stepped, and vanished.

"I'm here!" Alf squeaked.

Swinging around, Marcus saw Alf immediately behind him. But no sooner had he spotted him than the tree was off again, and Alf's squeak sounded even more plaintive. "I'm getting really dizzy, Mr. Prince. I don't know how much longer I can hang on . . ."

"You can do it! Hang on in there!" Marcus shouted. He took a deep breath, charged around the clearing, and flung himself at the tree's trunk. The tree remained perfectly still, and Marcus loosened his grip. With a twist and a slither, the birch was away, leaving Marcus with a badly scratched nose and empty arms. Scrambling to his feet, he looked wildly around. "Alf?"

There was no answer.

Marcus called again and stood still to listen. It was then that he became aware that the woods were very silent. Strangely silent. There was no birdsong, no rustling, not even the buzz of a bumblebee. It was as if time had stopped, and all Marcus could hear was his own breathing. Some sixth sense made him duck behind a thick clump of bracken, and his heart missed a beat as something landed on his shoulder.

"Kiddo," said a voice in his ear, "*freeze.*"

Marcus did as he was told.

The silence continued, but Marcus gradually realized that the earth beneath his feet was trembling. The trembling increased and turned into a steady thudding: *thud-thud-thud-thud-thud.* The thudding was followed by a shaking, until a shower of earth flew out of the hole in the center of the clearing, and a huge head emerged.

"Back! Go back, Clod! Back!" An elderly and very angry-looking dwarf popped up beside the head and began thumping it on one ear.

Clod blinked twice, said, "Yug!" and vanished.

"Master Amplethumb!" A second dwarf heaved himself out of the diggings and onto the grass, and began to dust the earth off his old brown jacket. "Master Amplethumb, excuse me for saying so—but you mustn't shout at the troll like that. It won't make him work any slower, and you might upset him . . . and there's an awful lot of him to get upset."

Master Amplethumb folded his arms and glowered. "But he won't stop, Bestius. He's already dug an entire new passage and turned the lower workings into rubble. He's knocked down half the roof supports, and I've had to send a team down to shore them up. And heaven knows where he's off to now."

Bestius pondered. "Why don't you take him down to the old mine? The one under the road to Flailing? You always said you could smell gold behind the rock face at the end. And that rock is pretty solid—digging there is sure to slow him down for a while."

Master Amplethumb's face cleared. "That's not a bad idea. And then, when he's done that, you can take him back."

"Ah." Bestius considered how best to break the news. "Well. I haven't really had time to explain it to you, but there might be a bit of difficulty. You see, King Thab wanted to make a deal."

"Of course he did," Master Amplethumb said impatiently. "What does he want? Gold? I told you he can have whatever he wants, as long as he doesn't mind waiting for it. Got to fulfill the palace order first."

"But he doesn't want gold." Bestius put his hands in his pockets. "He wants a princess."

"Eh?" Master Amplethumb stared. "What do you mean, he wants a princess?"

Bestius looked more and more uncomfortable. "He wants a princess to keep him company. A pretty princess. I . . . I happened to mention there'd be a whole lot of them at the wedding."

Master Amplethumb's mouth opened and shut several times, but no words came out. Finally he said, "Don't tell me . . . *please* don't tell me you agreed."

Bestius shrugged helplessly. "He'd never have sent the troll if I hadn't."

Master Amplethumb staggered backward, clutching his head. "Oh, my grandmother's whiskers," he said. "Oh, my granddaddy's bones. Whatever are we going to do? If we don't send Clod back, the trolls will be completely furious. It'll be war, no doubt about it. If we send him back but we don't send a princess with him, the trolls may not declare war, but it'll still be very nasty. And if we dare even to *suggest* to a princess that she might like to spend time with a huge, hairy troll, we'll have every single army from the entire Five Kingdoms after us." He paused and gave Bestius a solemn stare. "You've really gone and done it now."

Bestius bowed his head. "I thought you might be able to think of something. And there's a Council meeting tonight; I was going to raise the matter then."

Master Amplethumb snorted loudly. "Were you, indeed? Well, I'd say that'd be much too late. He'll have dug up half our best mines by then. No. I'm sorry, but there's only one thing to do. You, Bestius, will have to take that . . . that monster back and explain to King Thab that you didn't have the authority to make any such agreement, and the deal's off. We dwarves don't swap trolls for princesses. You'll have to persuade him to settle for a new crown, or a gold belt, or something sensible. Now come on. Your earth-moving machine's probably halfway underneath the Five Kingdoms by now." And Master Amplethumb climbed back into the hole and disappeared.

Bestius opened and shut his mouth, rubbed his nose, and pulled at his beard. "Oh, no, oh, no," he moaned. He sat down on the heap of freshly turned earth and put his head in his hands. "*What* am I going to do?"

Behind the bracken, Marlon and Marcus were in a state of shock. Marcus was reeling from the size of the troll; the wonder of seeing the dwarves paled beside the sight of Clod's enormous head, with its bulbous nose, massive ears, and tiny, blinking eyes. Wishing desperately that Gracie were there to share the experience, he had missed much of the conversation between Bestius and Master Amplethumb; Marlon, on the other hand, had heard every word. He too was reeling, but from the realization that his problems could be solved with astonishing ease. He coughed loudly, and the dwarf looked up.

"Who's that?"

"Got a plan," Marlon said as he flew out from behind the bracken, and Marcus was surprised to hear the jubilation in his voice. "Got a *good* plan. Bit of a bargain. You help us, and we'll help you."

"We?" Bestius stared at Marlon. "Who's *we*?"

Marlon coughed again. "Allow me to present my friend Prince Marcus, second in line to the Kingdom of Gorebreath." He swooped back behind the bracken and hissed, "Come out, kiddo! Want to rescue Gracie? Now's our chance!"

Chapter Seven

Princess Marigold was feeling exceptionally pleased with her achievements so far. She had tiptoed to the music-room door to check that Fedora was still busy trilling scales (with much enthusiasm but little accuracy), and then sped along the corridor to her sister's suite of rooms. There she had helped herself to Fedora's sky-blue dress covered in pink rosebuds. The dress was on the tight side—Marigold could never have been described as dainty—but determination and a certain amount of breath-holding achieved what had at first seemed impossible.

Flushed with excitement, Marigold had then hurried to the royal stables, where she was helped on her way by a stroke of good fortune. The head coachman had slipped off for half an hour to smoke an early-morning pipe with the head gardener, leaving the

youngest stable boy in charge. He was a small boy, easily intimidated, and when Marigold looked down her nose and informed him that she needed Fedora's pony and cart prepared as soon as possible because it was a matter of life and death and his job was on the line, he was only too happy to do as he was told. Ten minutes later she was bowling down the palace drive with a triumphant wave of her whip.

The stable boy hurried back into the yard, where he was met by an angry head coachman.

"Did I see Princess Marigold trundling off in the pony cart?" the coachman demanded.

The stable boy nodded. "Said it was urgent."

The coachman, who had known all the princesses since they were babies, snorted. "And I don't suppose you thought to ask where she was going? That's her sister's cart, that is, and I'd stake my best boots young Marigold never asked if she could take it. There'll be trouble; you mark my words."

Marigold was far from worrying about any trouble to come. She was humming happily as the pony trotted steadily onward, and from time to time she broke into cheerful and tuneless song. Queen Kesta had a leaden ear when it came to music, and her daughters were, if anything, even less gifted. Marigold had a repertoire of three notes, and it was sheer chance as to which she sang; this did not, however, stop her from enjoying herself hugely. "I'm the most beautiful princess in the whole wide world," she sang, "and I'm going to meet a handsome prince who will love me forever and ever. . . ."

A couple of local inhabitants heard her and rolled their eyes at each other.

"Let's hope he's deaf as a post," said one.

"Deaf as two posts," the other agreed.

Fortunately Marigold was out of earshot. The pony was going faster and faster in an effort to put as much distance as possible between himself and the wailing noise behind him; Marigold made several attempts to slow him down, but it was not until he broke into a gallop and she was scared into silence that he finally obeyed the frantic tugs on his reins. By that time they were all but at the border of the Five Kingdoms, and the pony was only too glad to walk at a more sedate pace as the well-made road gradually declined into a rough track.

The border itself was marked only by a couple of tall stone pillars, and Marigold looked around in wonder as she drove through. She had been expecting armed guards and high gates, or at the very least some kind of challenge, and was almost disappointed she had not had to talk her way into the land of unknown adventures. "Hmm," she said to herself. "I must remember to tell Mother. Anyone could get in! Horrible trolls and wicked witches and all sorts of nasty people . . . they could just march in any old time. There really should be at least a few soldiers."

Thinking about these unpleasant possibilities made Marigold feel less brave; it didn't help that the pony began to fling his head this way and that, as if he could sense something lurking behind the tangled bushes and tall, ivy-clad trees.

I hope Marcus comes soon, she thought. *I really don't want to wait here too long. Still, he's bound to think I'm very,* very *adventurous to come to such a scary place. Now, where shall I wait? I think . . . yes, I think I'll keep the pillars in sight.*

Marigold was pleased to find a shady half circle of birch trees; the grass beneath was soft and green and dotted with daisies, and she decided this would be an ideal setting for a romantic rescue. She pulled the pony to a halt, and after a few nervous glances this way and that, he began to graze. Marigold jumped out of the cart feeling that all was going according to plan. She had taken the precaution of bringing several satin and velvet cushions with her, and she arranged these carefully under the trees. "Three for me, and two for Marcus," she said, and patted them into place; after a moment's thought, she rearranged them rather closer together.

Pleased with the effect, she looked around to see what else needed to be done. There were wild roses growing in the hedge on the other side of the road-way, and it occurred to her that these would make a delightful wreath. Beaming, she hurried across the road and began to help herself. A moment later a sharp thorn embedded itself in her finger, and she screamed loudly. The pony flung up his head and stared around. Marigold was too busy trying to pull the thorn out of her finger to notice, and the pony took a few tentative steps back in the direction he had come. As nobody stopped him, he took a few more — and Marigold looked up.

"No!" she shrieked. "NO! Stay still! Don't move!"

The pony was used to Fedora coaxing him and petting him and telling him what a sweet, dear pony he was. He was not used to being shouted at, and he wasn't at all sure that he liked it. In fact, when he came to think about it, there wasn't much about the expedition so far that he *had* liked. No one had told him what a clever pony he was, no one had offered him oats or apples or a bucket of water, and there had been that dreadful caterwauling. As Marigold flung down her roses and rushed toward him, he thought of the rack of sweet-smelling hay in his stable and the handfuls of crunchy apples that Fedora would be sure to bring him, and he made up his mind. With a shake of his mane he was away, the cart bouncing and rattling behind him as he set off up the road at a gallop.

Marigold was left standing in the middle of the track, her injured finger in her mouth. "Stupid animal," she muttered—and then a thought popped into her mind. She had screamed. In fact, she had screamed very loudly. Surely Marcus ought to be dashing up to rescue her? Marigold frowned. Perhaps she should scream again? She stared up the track, but there was no sign of anyone. "Maybe it's too early," she said to herself.

She decided to give up on the roses and make a daisy chain instead, and wandered back to her cushions. Even the daisy chain was harder than she had expected, and after a few minutes she threw it down in disgust. Another ten minutes were spent in arranging herself in various different poses so she looked appealing, or sweet, or hopeful, but in the end she curled up and went to sleep.

Chapter Eight

Gracie Gillypot rubbed her eyes, then rubbed them again. The darkness was so incredibly dense that it made no difference whether her eyes were open or shut, and she began to wonder if she was real anymore. She pinched herself hard. "Ouch," she said out loud— then caught her breath. Had she heard a noise? "Hello? Is anybody there? Can you hear me?"

There was no answer.

Gracie sighed—then jumped. She had heard a sneeze—a very small sneeze, but nevertheless a sneeze, and it was enough to make her heart leap with a wild hope. "Marlon? Alf? Is that you?"

There was a second sneeze, before a snuffly voice asked, "Did you say Marlon? Do you mean Mr. Batster?"

"Oh, I do!" Gracie clasped her hands together. "Do you know him? Could you take him a message? Oh, please, that would be so wonderful. I don't know where I am, or how to get out of here!"

"I don't know him," the voice said. "I've just heard about him. I don't get out much." There was a crescendo of sneezing followed by the sound of fluttering wings. Gracie had the impression that the very small bat—if it was a bat—had sneezed itself off its perch and was having difficulty righting itself. "I'm going to have to go." The voice was reproachful now. "You're making me sneeze even more than usual."

"Oh, please don't go," Gracie begged. "Please stay. It's so terribly dark—and you sound like a very kind and helpful sort of"—she hesitated, then decided to risk it—"bat."

"Do you think so?" The bat sounded surprised. "Mostly they say I'm a waste of space. Always sneezing and all. It's not my fault, but they think it is. Never let me go flying with them, they don't." There was a small but heartfelt sigh. "'You stay right here in the tunnel, Flo,' they tell me. 'We don't want you grumbling and groaning and sneezing when we're out and about. Bats aren't meant to be noisy. You're best off at home where you can't be heard.' So I'm stuck here, day in and day out, and it's not fair. I mean, I know we've only just met, but you wouldn't say I was the complaining kind, would you?"

"Erm . . . certainly not." Gracie hesitated again. Something the bat had said had caught her attention. "Excuse me, but did you say we were in a tunnel?"

"Tunnel? Never!" Flo was indignant, but there was a clear note of alarm behind the outrage. "I never said anything of the sort! If anyone asks you, I never said anything about tunnels at all. No. No tunnels here. Not even one. I mean, that horrible Oolie creature would have me on toast if I started telling you dwarves about tunnels." Flo subsided into a fit of sniffing and snuffling.

Gracie considered what she'd heard. If she was in a tunnel, surely she should be able to find a way out—but it was obvious that she needed to be careful when asking Flo questions. "That's a really dreadful cold you've got," she said. "Have you had it long?"

"Oh, dearie, dearie, dearie me. If I've been asked that once, I've been asked a thousand times. It's not a cold! Understand? NOT a cold!"

Flo was now sounding angry, and Gracie bit her lip. The last thing she wanted was for the bat to fly away and leave her on her own. "I'm so sorry," she apologized. "Erm . . . might I ask if it's hay fever? If it is, the Ancient Crones have a wonderful potion that always cures it. One of Queen Kesta's daughters sneezed and sneezed and sneezed all summer long, and Auntie Edna cured her with just one spoonful. If . . . if you were to show me the way out, I could ask Auntie Edna to help you. You wouldn't need to be scared of her; I know people call her the Ancient One, and she's in charge of the web of power, but she's ever so kind. I promise it would work, and the crones are very fond of bats. . . ."

Gracie's voice died away. The silence was echoing all around her, and she was certain Flo had gone. She stretched out her arms and could feel nothing. Nothing but the terrible unrelenting blackness.

"Flo?" she called. "Flo? Oh, please don't leave me on my own!" Two large tears rolled down her cheeks, and the lump in her throat doubled in size. She fished in her pocket for a hankie and blew her nose hard before wiping her eyes and taking several deep breaths. "Come along, Gracie," she told herself. "It could be worse." She tried hard to think of what exactly could be worse than being stuck in a pitch-black tunnel with no idea where it led, or how to get out of it . . . and as she was thinking, she heard footsteps.

Weary, heavy, shuffling footsteps that were coming nearer. And nearer.

Gracie's stomach flipped, then froze. "Keep calm," she told herself. "Remember you're a Trueheart." She did her best, but however hard she tried, it was impossible not to wonder, "But what if whatever it is doesn't actually *know* about Truehearts? And what if it doesn't care? And what if it's hungry and has teeth?" She swallowed and took another deep breath. "Hello. Who's there?"

"'Tis Oolie, my little sweetmeat," said an ancient and quavering voice. "'Tis Oolie, and you've woken me up from my long, long sleep. Never did think as anything would come falling in here ever again, but there you is — and fine and delicious you do be smelling."

Cold shivers were running up and down Gracie's spine, but she forced herself to answer. "I'm so sorry if I woke you. I really am. I didn't mean to be here at all; I just sort of fell through a tree — and I'd be so very grateful if you could tell me the way out."

"But there's no getting out, my precious pudding." Oolie sounded so close that Gracie jumped. "Little dwarfies that fall into Oolie's trap don't ever get out again." There was a dry, dusty chuckle, and a long, bony finger poked Gracie in the ribs.

"But I'm not a dwarf," Gracie said as boldly as she could. "I'm a girl."

The rasping chuckle came again. "That's what they all used to say. 'I'm not a dwarfie—I'm a badger! I'm a little piggie! I'm a human being!' And did Oolie ever believe them? Oh, no, no, no. Oolie can smell dwarfies, cuz dwarfies is good little creatures, and you stinks of goodness. Much too good to be a greedy girlie, you is. Sniff-sniff-sniff, Oolie goes, and she can always tell."

Gracie twisted away from the probing finger. *Don't show her you're scared,* she told herself. *Stay calm. Think of . . . think of Auntie Edna.* Out loud she said, "But I AM a girl. I really truly am!"

There was a scratching noise, then the sound of something falling, and a muffled exclamation. This was followed by scuffling and much heavy and labored breathing before the scratching was repeated—and a light flared up. The contrast was so sudden and so bright that Gracie had to shut her eyes.

When she opened them, she saw that she was indeed in a tunnel, with walls of mud and closely intertwined tree roots. She had just enough time to discover that the light sprang from a tinderbox held by a hideously wrinkled old creature before it died again, and she was back in the all-enveloping darkness.

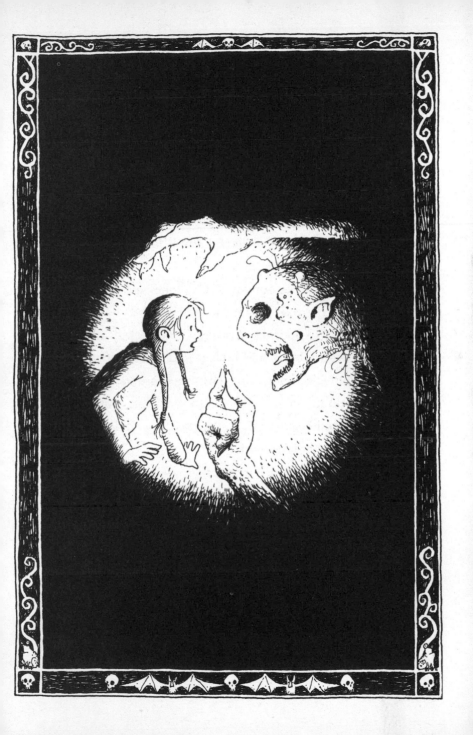

"Did . . . did you see?" she asked. "Could you see that I'm a girl? I promise you I am."

For a moment there was no answer, only the sound of puffing and wheezing. Then came more scratching, and the light flared up again. This time Oolie managed to light the small stump of a candle that was stuck onto one of the roots. The flame flickered, wavered, and then settled, and Gracie and Oolie stared at each other.

"So you *is* a human girl," Oolie said at last. She came very close to Gracie and sniffed at her. "But you smells good like dwarfies." She picked at her flat nose with a black and broken nail, then sniffed again. "And there's something else my nose is telling me. Something tingly." She licked her lips, sniffed once more, and began to pant. "Is you . . . could you be . . . is you . . . a Trueheart?"

Gracie opened her mouth to say yes—but a tiny flicker of movement caught her eye. A small bat was hanging by one claw immediately behind Oolie, vigorously shaking its head. Gracie changed her answer into a fit of coughing and then said, with all the conviction she could manage, "I think your nose might have made a mistake, Mrs. Oolie."

The creature gave her a suspicious look. "Is you

saying you isn't a Trueheart? Suppose I could be wrong. But tingles in the nose isn't dwarfies, even the goodest of dwarfies . . . and it isn't gnomies nor trolls neither."

"Gnomes?" Gracie pounced on the chance to turn the subject away from Truehearts. "I didn't know there were gnomes in the Five Kingdoms."

"But we *isn't* in the Kingdoms, is we, Miss Ignorant?" Oolie sneered. "We's under the forests, and there's all sorts down here in our tunnels and caverns. Take me, for instance. Half troll, half goblin, I is — strength of a troll with goblin brains — so don't you go thinking you can trick me. And what's more, it's Old Troll I be, hard as glass and strong as iron." She looked Gracie up and down, scratching thoughtfully at her balding head. "Looks to me like you's another mixamabody. Odd, you is, and no mistaking it. Now, if you *was* a Trueheart, that'd be worth a fortune to old Oolie . . . but if I takes you down Oolie's secret highways and byways to the King of All Trolls and you *isn't* a Trueheart after all, then what'll I get? Nothing. And Oolie's had too much nothing for years and years and years. . . ."

Gracie made no reply, although her mind was racing. It seemed that there was some kind of danger in being a Trueheart; did that mean she would be wise not to mention the Ancient Crones? There was no doubt that Oolie was evil; every time she came close, Gracie's skin felt cold and clammy. And what about Flo, the bat? She had retreated into the darkness beyond the candlelight, but it was just possible to pick out her shape against the tree roots. Was she trying to help? "She knew Marlon's name," Gracie told herself. "I've got to keep hoping for the best. . . . there's nothing else I can do."

Oolie gave Gracie one last stare, then nodded, as if she had come to a decision. "I knows who'll know. The Old Trolls can always smell out a Trueheart; been warring with them for years, they have. And Mullius Gowk's the oldest Old Troll of all. You come with me, Miss Oddity, and we'll find out what you really is, and if old Oolie's found her fortune." And she seized Gracie's wrist with one hand, picked up the candle with the other, and began dragging Gracie along the tunnel.

Gracie was astonished at the old creature's strength; her wrist felt as if it were encircled by an iron band, and she realized that it would be hopeless to try to twist out of Oolie's grasp even if she had any idea of where to run. But where was she being taken? And who was she going to meet?

"I'll blow out the candle," breathed a tiny voice in

her ear. "She'll have to light it again, and she'll need two hands. When she lets go of you, turn and run back the way you've come. Quiet as you can."

Before Gracie could answer, there was a muffled sneeze and a flutter of wings, and the candle was extinguished. Oolie muttered angrily, then gave Gracie's arm a sharp and painful tug. Gracie lost her balance and fell heavily, and Oolie growled a furious growl.

"Ouch!" Gracie's knees were in agony, and her hand was bruised and sore. "Ouch, ouch, ouch!" Her wails were so genuine that Oolie stopped trying to haul her along and tried instead to heave her back on her feet, but without success. Gracie's legs had turned to jelly, and she was quite unable to stand.

"Stay still!" Oolie ordered. "Don't move, or I'll bite you!" And she let go of Gracie's wrist.

For a moment Gracie was too stunned to move, but then there was a flurry of wings and sneezing and a furious yell, and it was evident that Flo was harrying Oolie as she tried to light the candle. Gracie gritted her teeth and tried to get up. There was something hard under her hip; with a start she realized it was the tinderbox, and she slipped it into her pocket before forcing herself to stand. Then, with one hand on the side of the tunnel and the other stretched out in front of her, she began to half run, half limp as fast as she could, back the way she had come. Behind her she heard cursing and swearing, and finally the sound she was dreading most — the sound of shuffling footsteps.

"Hurry, Trueheart — hurry!" Flo was squeaking at her loudest, urging her on, and Gracie did her best to increase her speed. She was puffing too hard to hear the footsteps come to a sudden stop, as if their owner had heard something of immense interest. Nor did she notice when they began again — this time going in the opposite direction.

Chapter Nine

Princess Fedora of Dreghorn, soon to be married with bells and doves and hearts and every other romantic decoration that could be obtained from Madam Millicent's Royal Emporium, was furious. Once her singing lesson was over and the music teacher had unblushingly assured her that she had the voice of an angel, a lark, and a fluting thrush, she had decided to have just one more peek at her wedding dress . . . a truly delicious sky-blue dress with little pink rosebuds. But on opening her wardrobe she had found it gone—and nobody could tell her who had taken it. Further investigation revealed that her sister Marigold was also missing; putting the two facts together led Fedora to the obvious conclusion.

"Mother!" she shrieked as she burst in through the door of Queen Kesta's private sitting room. "It's just too, *too* awful of Marigold! She's miles and miles and *miles* fatter than me and she'll absolutely ruin my beautiful dress and I HATE her!"

The queen, who was having her morning cup of coffee with the dowager duchess and their mutual friend Queen Bluebell of Wadingburn, looked up in surprise. "Whatever do you mean, my sweet child?"

Fedora stamped her foot in a distinctly unprincessy way. "It's that horrible Marigold. She's stolen my wedding dress, and she'll ruin it—I just *know* she will, because she's fat, fat, FAT!"

Queen Kesta's large blue eyes opened wide. "Dearest one," she remonstrated, "that isn't at all a polite way of expressing yourself. I'm sure if Marigold has borrowed your dress—which I rather doubt—it's only so she can . . ." The queen's imagination failed to supply a reason, and she looked at her friends for support.

"So she can choose ribbons to match," Queen Bluebell suggested.

Queen Kesta beamed. "Exactly so!"

Fedora folded her arms and glowered. "She wouldn't do that. She's wanted it ever since I got it. She thinks it'll make Marcus think she's pretty, as if a silly, fat pig like her could ever—"

"HUSH, dear!" Queen Kesta held up her hands in horror. "That's quite enough! Look—you've made your dear great-aunt choke over her coffee with your horrid remarks about your poor little sister."

Queen Bluebell banged Hortense on the back with such enthusiasm that the duchess all but fell over. Recovering her balance, she stopped choking and blew her nose. It had occurred to her that it was just possible that Marigold had taken her advice about going on an adventure, and she was wondering how much she should say. She was both impressed and appalled that Marigold had the temerity to steal her sister's wedding dress; this was something Hortense had not anticipated. It certainly showed great determination if Marigold had decided to dress the part before setting out to find her prince. Or was she jumping to entirely the wrong conclusions? It was perfectly possible that Marigold was merely skulking in one of the hundreds of palace bedrooms, twirling around and around in front of a gilded mirror and admiring herself enormously. Hortense blew her nose for the second time and decided to await developments.

Queen Kesta was trying hard to think of a way to improve Fedora's temper. "Why don't we go for a little walk in the gardens, dear one?" she suggested.

"Or you could show us that sweet pretty pony of yours. I don't think you've seen him yet, have you, Bluebell? Or you, Auntie?"

The duchess smiled. "No. No, I've not seen the pony. That would be delightful." If what she was beginning to suspect was indeed the case, it would be extremely interesting to have a look in the royal stables.

Queen Kesta, pleased to see Fedora beginning to look more cheerful, heaved herself to her feet and bustled her guests out of her sitting room and down the splendid marble staircase. Fedora hung back to fill her pockets with sugar lumps, then followed her mother and her companions as they crossed the black-and-white checkered marble hall to go out into the drive leading to the royal stables. Once outside, Fedora hurried ahead while Queen Kesta took the opportunity to tell Hortense and Bluebell how well Fedora drove her pony cart, and how she hoped that when Fedora was married she would drive over to visit at least three times a week.

"Good idea," Queen Bluebell said heartily. "Nice to keep in touch. Hope my granddaughter, Loobly, does the same when she gets hitched. Don't care so much about Vincent. Silly boy. Does nothing but sit around. Needs a quest. Don't suppose you know of anything, do you, Hortense? Seem to remember you were a bit of an adventurer in your time."

The dowager duchess was saved from replying by a piercing scream, followed by a short silence, then several agonized squeals. Queen Kesta went pale and clutched at Bluebell's arm. "What is it?" she said with a gasp. "Who is it?" In her agitation the queen lost all sense of punctuation and became almost incomprehensible: "Whatever could have happened we must hurry and see oh my goodness gracious could it be my darling precious daughter has been hurt?"

At that moment Fedora appeared, her face scarlet with rage, dragging the stable boy behind her by one ear. "Mother! *Mother!* You've got to throw this horrible boy in the dungeon this MINUTE! He let Marigold take my pony and cart and he never tried to stop her, and I'll hate Marigold forever and ever and *ever* for this, and don't think I'll forgive her because I WON'T. And what's more, I wouldn't let her be my bridesmaid now if she were the last girl left on earth!" Then she burst into a furious fit of weeping and threw herself on her mother's ample chest.

It was left to Hortense and Queen Bluebell to question the stable boy, and Hortense quickly discovered that she had been right in her suspicions. Princess Marigold of Dreghorn had broken with every royal tradition and had gone on an adventure.

Well, well, well, the duchess thought as Bluebell reassured the boy that he had done nothing more than his duty by obeying Princess Marigold's orders, and that the dungeon would remain empty. *Well, well, well! Maybe there's more to that girl than I thought. . . . Let's hope it's all worth it, and she finds her prince!*

She did not mention this thought to either Queen Kesta or Fedora. Fedora was still weeping copiously, and Queen Kesta had just realized that Marigold had run away. The stable boy, when questioned, had no idea where the princess might have gone, and the queen became more and more hysterical—until at last Queen Bluebell stepped forward and boomed, "Silence!"

Even Fedora stopped wailing, and she, her mother, and her great-aunt looked at the queen in astonishment.

"Sorry if I shouted," Bluebell said without any sign of being sorry at all. "Had to stop you, Kesta dear. No good shrieking like that. No good getting the army involved, either; the girl won't have come to any harm. No—if she's gone off in frills and finery, there'll be a boy involved, you take my word for it. I'd say she's eloped, and good luck to her."

This was not a helpful suggestion; Queen Kesta immediately collapsed in a heap of skirts and petticoats and began to weep piteously. Fedora, realizing that the attention had moved away from her, joined in.

Great-Aunt Hortense sighed. She was going to have to own up. She hauled her niece to her feet and said, "She hasn't eloped, Kesta. *Kesta?* Can you hear me? She has NOT eloped. She's gone to the border of the Five Kingdoms, and I can assure you that she won't go more than a step or two beyond."

Marigold's devoted mother turned to the duchess, her bosom heaving. "Hortense! How do you know? Why ever would she go there?"

"Because," Hortense explained, "I suggested it."

Queen Kesta was, for once in her life, entirely speechless. She stared at her aunt while she tried to find the words to express her horror and indignation.

Before she could speak, however, Queen Bluebell clapped her hands and roared with laughter. "Well done, Hortense! I knew you were a wild one! An adventure will do the girl a world of good. Too much mollycoddling of princesses these days, too much by half. But don't you worry about young Marigold!" Bluebell looked triumphant. "I've worked it all out.

I'll send my Vincent to find her; it's exactly what he needs. Can't send him riding after her on a snow-white steed, I'm afraid—don't have one, and besides, he'd fall off. No, I'll send him in my royal carriage. He'll find your girl, rescue her, and bring her home safely. That'll make them both happy. She'll have her adventure, and he'll feel useful for once. Never know—they might even fall in love! But I'd better be off. No time to be wasted, although the longer Marigold has to wait, the more pleased she'll be to see Vincent. And I'll make sure there's a hamper of goodies in the coach—nothing like a nice picnic to set two young things off on the right path. No need to thank me—the pleasure's all mine!" And Queen Bluebell waved a regal wave and set off at a quick march toward her waiting carriage.

"Oh," Queen Kesta said, and she sank down onto a convenient step. "Oh . . ."

Hortense sat down beside her and put a comforting arm around her niece's shoulders. "I'm sorry, Kesta dear. I never thought Marigold would take me seriously. But I do think Bluebell's plan might solve the problem rather neatly. I really do."

"Hmph." Fedora folded her arms. "We'll see. They're both horrible, so I suppose they'll suit each other.

Mother, can I have a new dress? Rose-pink with blue roses? Only with more petticoats than the last one?"

Her mother, who was wondering if she was in the middle of some strange and dreadful dream, nodded feebly. "Of course, dearest. But now I think I *must* have a cup of tea. Auntie dear, could you help me up?"

Chapter Ten

Gubble was making steady, if slow, progress. A solid and determined troll, he took the most direct route to Flailing and the Unreliable Forest; if trees or bushes got in his way, he either rooted them up or squashed them flat. When at last he saw Marcus's pony patiently standing beside the pathway, he grunted and began to peer around to see if Marcus was nearby. After ten minutes he had still found no sign of the prince, and no sign of any dwarf activity either. Gubble scratched his head and tried to think what he should do next. Thinking was not something he found easy. After a while he fixed his gaze on Glee, some faint idea stirring in his small and dusty mind about animals having the ability to follow their masters' tracks. "Marcus!" he instructed. "Find Marcus!"

Glee looked at the troll but did not move. He was not at all unhappy to have Gubble's company; the trees around him had stopped their sneering and whispering as the troll approached. The pony was deeply loyal, however, and Marcus had told him to stay where he was. Gubble came closer.

"Gracie in danger," he explained. "Go! Us find Marcus."

Glee's ears twitched, and he lowered his head and whickered softly. Gubble nodded. "Good. Good! Now find Marcus." He took hold of the reins and tugged Glee toward the track so as to encourage him. It was unfortunate that Gubble was quite unaware of his own strength; the pony shot forward, staggered, and in trying to save himself, lurched heavily against the troll. Gubble's head, never firmly attached even at the best of times, fell off. With a terrified whinny and a wild shake of his mane, Glee set off down the track at a gallop, and Gubble was left rolling on the muddy ground with his feet in the air. "Ug," he said crossly. "Ug."

It took Gubble some time, but at last he was re-assembled. His head had been bumped and shaken by its fall, and he found a new idea was rattling around inside. "Prints!" he announced, and felt a warm glow of pride sweep over him. "Footprints."

Fired up by his cleverness, he stomped purposefully along the path in the opposite direction from that taken by Marcus's pony. Here and there the ground was damp and muddy, and Gubble gave a grunt of excitement when he finally saw two clear sets of footprints: one larger, made by an expensive pair of riding boots, and a smaller pair, rather scuffed around the heels.

"Clever Gubble," he congratulated himself, and increased his speed to a shambling run. When a birch tree made a sudden sideways leap across the path, it caught him completely by surprise, and for the second time in ten minutes his head left his body. This time it rolled under a large gorse bush; his nose was prickled by thorns, his mouth was filled with leaves, and his angry mutters sent a family of beetles running for cover.

"It's OK, Mr. Troll," said a squeaky voice. "I can see it! Stop pulling those branches to bits, and I'll tell you where to look. I mean, I'll tell you where to put your hand."

Gubble stopped quivering with rage, and from under the bush his disembodied voice said, "Alf?"

"That's right," said the little bat. "Move your hand left—no, *left*! The other way . . . that's right. I mean, that's the way to move it. Just a little bit farther— there! Well done!"

Gubble hauled his head back toward him and thunked it into place on his shoulders. A wisp of silver thread was draped over one ear, and he pulled it off—but then, seeing it was pretty and thinking that Gracie might like it, he tied it clumsily around his wrist.

"Better now?" Alf inquired from his perch on a nearby twig.

"Ug," Gubble said with feeling. "Thank." And then, "Where Marcus?"

Alf waved a wing. "Over there. He's waiting for Marlon to come back and tell him what to do. Did you know that Gracie disappeared?" Alf puffed out his extremely small chest. "I'm marking the tree she fell through."

"Tree?" Gubble stared at him. "What tree?"

"*This* tree. But it keeps trying to move, and it's getting really hard to hang on. I don't suppose you could hold on to it for me while I have a rest?"

Gubble's answer was to take firm hold of the slender silver birch. He felt a shiver under his arms and a quivering. A moment later, twiggy fingers clutched him, and Alf, watching wide-eyed from above, saw the troll's solid body vanish. There was nothing to show that he had ever been there at all, nothing except for a sizable bulge in the birch tree's trunk. And a sudden sound that made Alf giggle.

Chapter Eleven

If anybody had told Marcus that he would spend a whole hour having an argument with a bat in front of a confused dwarf, he would not have believed them. "But Marlon," he said for the umpteenth time, "I can't get hold of a princess just like that. It just won't happen. You've seen them; you know what they're like. Stupid, the lot of them. Even if I knocked one senseless and carted her here by force, she'd scream her head off the minute she woke up. And they're terrified of trolls. Honestly — if I even mention the word, they go into spasms and screech for hours. Idiotic, or what? I mean, I know that thing we saw just now was huge, but it wasn't exactly dangerous — and Gubble's one of my best friends."

Marlon considered explaining to Marcus that not all trolls were like Gubble, but he decided to leave that for another time.

"Seems simple enough to me, kiddo. No problemo re: the screaming—trolls are used to it. And look at it my way: one princess for the dwarves equals they dig our Gracie out." He turned to Bestius. "Right? If we get you a dame, you'll help us?"

Bestius blinked, considered briefly, then nodded.

"Sorted." Marlon waved a wing. "So it's up to you, kid. . . ."

Marcus groaned and put his head in his hands.

Bestius, who had been imagining the most appalling future for himself and all the dwarves as the result of his foolish promise, saw the possibility of a solution hanging in the balance. He too had realized how little Marcus knew about trolls, and he also did not feel this was the right moment to enlighten the prince. "She wouldn't have to *stay*," he suggested. "If we could just hand her over for even an hour or so, we'll have honored our . . ." He stopped and looked embarrassed. "I mean, *my* promise. King Thab'll have no excuse to take revenge on us dwarves, and we can get on with our work." He gave Marcus a cool stare. "And while we're talking about work, I'd like to point out that if you Royals hadn't insisted on so many crowns for the Dreghorn wedding, we'd never have gotten into this situation in the first place."

"True enough," Marlon agreed. His eyes brightened. "Hey, kiddo! Here's a plan! You get hold of the dame; our friend here trots her off to the trolls; the king gets happy. The dwarves dig out Gracie; we get happy. And—listen to this, kid! While the dwarves are busy with our Gracie, *you* rescue the princess from the trolls—and hey! You're a hero!"

Marcus sat up and looked thoughtful. The role of hero had a strong appeal. His life so far had been safe, privileged, and exceptionally boring, whereas Gracie—in Marcus's view, a romantically aban-doned orphan—had survived a terrible childhood and had already had several interesting adventures. Admittedly he had shared in a couple of these, but he never felt that he had covered himself in glory. Marcus looked at the hopeful faces of Marlon and Bestius and went on thinking. He would happily dig Gracie out of her imprisonment with his bare hands if that were practical, and he would be just as happy to do battle with any enemy that threatened her, but standing to one side while a team of dwarves rescued her was not in any way heroic. On the other hand, saving the dwarves from a war with the trolls followed by rescuing a princess from a troll king would really be something . . . a genuine adventure. And there was an additional attraction, now that he came to think of it. Surely his father would be impressed by such real heroism—even, perhaps, sufficiently impressed to excuse Marcus from taking part in the hideous royal wedding. Ignoring the fact that he himself would be responsible for putting the princess in danger in the first place, Marcus made a decision.

"OK," he said—and Marlon and Bestius sighed in relief. "I'll go. Don't know how I'll do it, but I will. But on one condition, and one condition only. It'll take me a while to get to Dreghorn and sweet-talk one of those stupid girls into coming back with me, and I can't leave Gracie stuck wherever she is until then. The dwarves must start work on getting her out right now. Hey! Is Alf still marking the tree? Didn't he disappear?"

"We'll sort it out, kiddo," Marlon reassured him.

"I'll be off, then." Marcus stood at attention, saluted, then bowed to Bestius. "You have the word of Prince Marcus of Gorebreath." And he hurried off through the trees.

Bestius looked after him, rubbing his chin. "No offense, but is he a reliable sort of a lad? I don't want to dig this girl out and then have him say, 'Ho-di-ho! Let's forget all about this princess business.' You know what humans are like. All promises and no payment."

Marlon drew himself up to his full height of six inches. "Told you before," he said grandly. "That lad is Prince Marcus. One cool dude. Honorable from top to toe."

"Beg pardon, I'm sure." Bestius shrugged. "I'll take your word for it. So where do we start digging?"

"We find my nephew—we find the tree. Easy as pie." Delighted by the success of his plan, Marlon waved a confident wing. "He's on the case. Trust me, he's—"

The rest of his sentence was interrupted by a wild squeaking as Alf arrived at top speed and hurled himself at his uncle. "Unc! It's happened again! The tree! It's got the troll! Vanished, just perzactly like Miss Gracie! Gone! What'll we do?"

"Troll?" Bestius's eyebrows rose. "What troll?"

Marlon disentangled himself from his nephew and dusted himself off. "Keep cool, kid. Keep cool. Tell it slowly. . . ."

Alf took a deep breath and steadied himself. "It's Gubble, Uncle Marlon. His head fell off, and I found it for him, and then I asked him to hang on to the tree Miss Gracie fell into because I was getting so tired and dizzy, and then—*whoomph!* He was gone too! And I didn't know what to do, so I came to find you."

His uncle gave him an unsympathetic glare. "Alfred Batster," he said coldly, "are you telling me you've left that tree unmarked?"

Alf shook his head. "It's OK. It's not moving anymore, Unc. Ever since it ate Gubble, it's been keeping very, very still — and it's got hiccups."

Bestius and Marlon stared at the small bat. "Hiccups?" Bestius said at last. *"Hiccups?"*

Alf nodded. "Follow me, and I'll show you. Oh, Uncle Marlon, do you think Gubble will rescue Miss Gracie? Will it end happily ever after, after all?"

"I think," Marlon said carefully, "we'd better have a look at this tree."

Chapter Twelve

In the dark, cavernous throne room, deep beneath the forests beyond the Five Kingdoms, King Thab was waiting for his princess. Spittle eyed him thoughtfully as Thab paced around and around.

Mullius was also watching the king. He had always been of the opinion that any female, be she princess or troll, was a bad idea and must be gotten rid of as soon as possible. Females caused trouble. Arguments. Confusion. Thab was not like the High Kings of old, who had regularly dragged their wives and sweethearts over rocks by the hair if they showed signs of disobedience. He was, in Mullius's view, a mere puppet, and the arrival of a human princess would make him even more feeble. The Old Troll flexed his muscles, and the chain attached to his wrist rattled.

King Thab glanced around at the noise and stopped

his pacing. He stomped toward the iron box and stood staring down at it. At last he said, "Key!"

Spittle scrambled down from his perch behind the massive throne, convinced he had misheard. "I beg your pardon, Your Majesty? What did you say?"

"Key!" The king pointed to a large bunch of iron keys hanging on a hook by the heavily barred door.

The goblin nodded and ran to fetch them. Mullius growled deep in his chest, but he made no move as the king took the keys and pointed to the door.

"Go," the king ordered. Mullius still made no move, and Thab frowned. "Go!" he repeated. He turned to Spittle and waved an imperious arm. "Go too."

Spittle bowed. "Of course, Your Majesty. And when shall we come back? That is, I assume you do want us to come back? I trust this isn't a termination of our employment . . ."

King Thab shook his heavy head. "Thab will call. Go!"

"Ah!" The goblin did his best to hide his relief. "I see. You wish to be alone with your box. Of course. How tactless of us. Come, Mullius." And the goblin gave the massive bulk of the Old Troll a helpful push. Mullius roared with anger, then roared again as the door crashed shut behind him and the wooden bar thudded into place.

Alone in the throne room, King Thab turned the bunch of keys around in his scaly hands until he found the one he wanted. Bending down, he carefully unlocked a small cupboard underneath his throne, and from the cupboard took a curiously twisted key. This he slotted into the lock on the iron box—but he did not turn it. Instead, he lowered himself to the stone floor and sat very still for a long time.

"Pretty princess," he murmured at last. "Pretty princess. Be special king for pretty princess." He took a deep breath, turned the key, and lifted the lid. Inside was a piece of thick black velvet; Thab moved it away and was almost dazzled by what lay beneath. Gleaming and glittering even in the low light of the cavern, a heart of glass lay on its soft velvet bed.

"Aaaaaah," breathed the king, and he placed one hand on the heart and one on his chest. "Aaaaaah . . ."

"Mind you, don't break it," Oolie said from right behind him. "Precious sort of thing, that is."

As the king swung around, rage, surprise, and fear written all over his face, she held up a protective arm. "Now, don't you go hurting old Oolie. Oolie might have news for you, news that'll make you happy." She squatted down, her small black eyes glinting. "Guess what Oolie caught today in her little old trap."

King Thab moved to cover the heart with the piece of velvet, but Oolie caught his hand in a grip of iron.

"Not so fast, my dearie. Guess first!"

The king considered throwing her against the wall, but there was something in her eyes that reminded him of the way Mullius looked at him; a look suggesting a lack of respect—contempt, even. Unwilling to risk a full-blown battle of wills, he decided to humor her. "Rabbit," he said. "Goblin. Dwarf . . ." He paused as Oolie shook her head.

She tapped her nose and grinned, showing her broken teeth, sharp as needles. "Better," she hissed. "Much better."

The heart shifted a little in its velvet-lined box, throwing sharp sparkles of light across the dark and dirty ceiling. King Thab shut his eyes tightly, then opened them. "Trueheart?" he whispered, hardly daring to believe he was saying the word. "Not . . . Trueheart?"

Oolie nodded. "Trueheart it is." Distracted by its dazzle, she peered at the heart. "So that'll be the High King's lost heart, then." She gave a long, low whistle. "Had it long, have you?"

King Thab did his best to look superior. "Grandfather got treasure box. Hush! Hush! Secret! Grandfather gave it Father. Father gave it me. Only royal kings know secret in box."

"Ooooh! Royal, is you?" Oolie sneered. "I heard as your grandpappy got to be king by snake's-tongue words and power of poison. Nothing to do with the High King, was he?"

"Who you?" Thab stared at her, his face scarlet with suppressed anger. "How get in? Doors shut — big bars. Bolts!"

Oolie swung herself from foot to foot, chuckling sourly. "Oolie has her ways. Been hiding and sliding for hundreds of years, Oolie has, since the Old Trolls was sent away . . . but you never knew as I was here, did you?"

King Thab shook his head.

"Come from the Old Trolls, I does, and the old ones never trusted anyone. If there was a lock, they'd set a spy to watch it . . . and a secret door to slither and slide through — but you wouldn't know that, poor thing that you is."

For a moment it seemed as if Oolie had gone too far; Thab let out a mighty roar and sprang at her, fully intending to throttle her with his bare hands. Oolie, agile despite her age, slid out of his reach behind the throne. "Isn't you wanting to hear about the Trueheart, then?" she mocked.

Panting, the king stood still. "Tell!"

Oolie grinned an unpleasant grin. "What'll you give poor old Oolie in exchange for telling? Gold? A fireside? Food and warmth for the rest of my days?"

"Yes!" The king nodded. "Yes! Where Trueheart now?"

"Oh, she's safe enough, she is. Thinks she's about to get out with a silly little bat to show her the way. A silly little bat who squeaks loud enough for old Oolie to hear . . ." Oolie rubbed her hands together with glee. "But Oolie's traps is good traps. There's no way out, no way out at all. Not the way she's running. She'll come to the end, then *wham-slam*! Caught, she'll be, cuz Oolie's traps is sneaky. Nasty, they is. Double sprung, with a twist at the end. Mullius Gowk, he'll tell you of my traps. Many a dwarfie-pie he ate when he was young, and all of them caught by Oolie." She gave a high-pitched cackling laugh and licked her lips.

King Thab looked at her uneasily.

"No eat dwarves now. Laws say no. No eat dwarves."

"More's the pity!" Oolie snapped. She pointed at the glittering heart. "The High King'd eat them two at a time. Crunch their bones, then pick the beard hairs out of his teeth." She gave Thab a calculating look.

"So . . . so what was you thinking of doing with my Trueheart, then?"

King Thab stood up straight and thrust out his chest. "Is story. Old story. 'When Trueheart life . . .'" He hesitated, searching for the words.

"I knows that story, my dearie dear," Oolie said in a softer tone. "The old ones sang it when Oolie was in her cradle, long, long ago. Shall Oolie say it for you?"

"Yes! Yes! Say!" The king clapped his hands.

Oolie began to chant:

"When Trueheart's life is ended here,
the High King's heart will beat once more
and power come to those who reign.
A King of Kings will rule again."

"Good!" King Thab stamped his foot in excitement. "King of Kings! Thab be King of Kings! Great king, like High King. Then . . ." His small eyes began to glow. "Pretty princess will love Thab when Thab is King of Kings!"

Oolie chuckled silently. *So that's the way of it,* she thought. She got off the throne and made an obsequious bowlegged curtsy. "You will be King of Kings indeed, my dearie. And Oolie will give up her home to help pretty princess, because pretties need a lady friend, as you well knows." She came a little closer and adopted a wheedling tone. "Promise you'll let old Oolie stay and make the pretty one happy, my dear. You'll be all-powerful, just like it says in the story."

"Power! Yes! Can make new rules! New laws!" King Thab thundered across the room and ripped the notice about a smile a day from the wall. "All will listen to Thab! Dwarves, goblins, human kings—all will bow!"

"Don't feel too certain of yourself, does you?" Oolie was unable to keep a jeering note out of her voice. "Is that why you went along with all those contracts and suchlike? 'Fraid folk'd find out your grandpappy was nothing more than the High King's servant—not even one of the Old Trolls . . . ?"

Thab's eyes dimmed, and his shoulders drooped. He picked up the torn notice and began to straighten it before turning back to Oolie. "Am king," he said flatly. "King Thab."

"But you'll soon be King of Kings . . . just as long as Oolie helps you." Oolie sidled up and gave him an ingratiating smile. "Promise you'll always look after your friend Oolie. Promise you'll put it in writing, so's all can see. 'Oolie to be your true friend, and always companion of the pretty princess.' Then Oolie will find you the Trueheart."

King Thab nodded and looked more cheerful. "Yes," he said. "End Trueheart life. Power for King Thab!" He bent to wrap the heart of glass in the black velvet — but as the material touched the glimmering surface, there was a hiss and a puff of smoke. The velvet shriveled and turned to ashes. The king jumped back, alarmed, and Oolie cackled loudly.

"Seems you've woken something that doesn't want to sleep again." She stretched out a long, sinewy arm and pushed at the box's iron lid. It clanged into place; King Thab tried to turn the key, but it would not move. "Best leave it as it is," Oolie advised. "Now, let's get that promise in writing, shall us, my dearie? Oolie can write. Clever, she is."

To Oolie's frustration, the king ignored her. He gave the box a doubtful glance, then marched to unbar the door.

Spittle was hovering outside, a curious expression on his face. "What can I do for you, Your Majesty?"

"Get Mullius," King Thab ordered. "Mullius find Trueheart. *Now!*"

Oolie leaped forward. "But is *Oolie's* Trueheart! Oolie will fetch . . ."

King Thab looked at her and grunted. "No. Show the way."

Before Oolie could reply, the goblin gave her a mocking glance. "He won't trust anyone but Mullius, dear madam. I suggest you do as you're told." He scurried toward the doorway. "Mullius! MULLIUS!"

As Mullius made his way back into the room, he greeted Oolie without surprise, giving her a sullen nod. When Thab told him the Trueheart was heading toward one of Oolie's dwarf-traps, however, the Old Troll's eyes shone with a greedy gleam. "Mullius know all traps," he said. "Mullius find Trueheart."

Oolie dug her talon-like nails into her palms. In her boastfulness, she had said too much. "What of Oolie?" she wailed. "You'll not forget old Oolie, will you? 'Twas Oolie as catched the Trueheart, 'twas Oolie as told you . . ."

But the king wasn't listening. Oolie moved slowly backward, and her hand slid over the back of the enormous throne. A tweak on a cunningly concealed lever, and she was gone. King Thab, intent on sending Mullius on his mission, did not notice.

Chapter Thirteen

In the darkness of the tunnel, Gracie was trying not to panic. Her outstretched hands could feel nothing but solid earth in front of her. "Flo!" she whispered. "I can't go on! What shall I do?"

There was a fluttering and a sneeze, then Flo's small voice said, "Turn sharp to the right, Trueheart. Be careful."

Gracie did as she was told, and her exploring fingers found the narrow entrance to a smaller tunnel. As she felt her way inside, a breath of fresh air touched her face. "Oh! This must be the way out!" she exclaimed, and she was about to take a joyful stride forward when the bat squeaked loudly and fluttered across her face.

"Wait! Stop! I've made a mistake! It's no good!"

"No good?" Gracie asked. "What do you mean?"

A thought struck her, and she fished in her pocket for the tinderbox. It took her a moment or two to make it work, but when the sparks finally flew in the air, she gasped. In front of her was a narrow tunnel leading upward, with the faintest glimmer of daylight at the far end—but if she had rushed into it, as every part of her longed to do, she would have fallen into a pit so deep she was unable to see the bottom. "Oh," Gracie breathed as she leaned against the wall to recover. "Flo, you're a hero. If I'd fallen in there, I'd never have gotten out again. Not ever, and it would have been much, *much* worse than being in a tunnel"—she shivered—"even with that horrible Oolie person chasing me . . . but I think she's gone away now, thank goodness."

Flo sneezed several times in quick succession. "But she might be up to something." She sneezed again, and Gracie wondered if the little bat sneezed whenever she was anxious. "Do you know much about trolls?"

Gracie was beginning to say that one of her very best friends was a troll when a vibration in the wall beside her made her jump. The vibration became a shaking, and a large chunk of earth fell with a thud close to Gracie's feet. Her mouth went dry, and for a terrible moment she thought Oolie was about to leap on her. Instead there was another fall of earth, followed by the sound of a heavy body crashing to the ground. Gracie was frozen with fear; she held her breath, hoping against hope that nobody could hear the sound of her heart hammering in her chest.

"Ug," said a familiar voice. "Ug."

"Gubble?" Gracie's eyes filled with grateful tears. "Gubble? Is that you?"

"Is," said Gubble, and Gracie stumbled toward him and hugged as much of him as she could find in the darkness.

"Oh, Gubble," she said, "oh, Gubble — I'm so pleased to see you!"

"Gubble pleased too." Gracie could tell he was smiling his widest smile. "Gubble fell. Gubble went bump." There was a pause. "Gubble lost head."

Gracie pulled the tinderbox out, and by the light of a flurry of sparks she inspected the troll. "No, you haven't," she said. "It's just where it ought to be. On your shoulders. Gubble, let me introduce you to Flo — she's the most wonderful bat. She saved me from falling into a horrible pit! Flo — Flo? Where are you?"

Flo, who had been lurking in the side tunnel, sneezed and fluttered onto Gracie's shoulder. "What sort of troll is that?" she asked.

"This is the friend I was telling you about," Gracie explained. "He must have come to rescue me." She found Gubble's hand and held it tightly. "Gubble, I've promised Flo that the crones will cure her hay fever, so we've all got to get out of here together. How did you get in? Can we get out the same way? Oh—I do wish that we could *see* each other." She sent another stream of sparks flying from the tinderbox and was delighted to see one of Oolie's candle ends stuck in a shallow cavity in the wall. A moment later it was burning steadily, and she heaved a sigh of relief. "That's better. So—how can we get out?"

"Gubble fell through tree," Gubble announced. He turned around, but the wall behind him showed no sign that it had ever been disturbed. He looked puzzled. "Came that way. Where hole now?"

"That's how I got here," Gracie told him. "I fell down at first, but then I slid sideways. It's like a secret door in the side of the tunnel, but it's really a dwarf-trap—isn't that right, Flo?"

Flo was shifting uneasily on Gracie's shoulder. "That's right. But you should get out of here as

soon as you can. It's dangerous—especially for you, Trueheart."

"Why? What's wrong with being a Trueheart?" Gracie asked.

There was a wild flurry of sneezing before Flo could reply. "I don't exactly know . . . but . . ." She began sneezing so uncontrollably that Gracie took her in her cupped hands and began to smooth her fur.

"Hush," she soothed, "hush . . ."

"It's the trolls!" Flo gasped between sneezes. "I've heard them talking, and my brothers and sisters have heard things too." Her sneezes overcame her again, and it was a couple of minutes before she could go on. "There's something about Truehearts and trolls, and it's not good, not good at all. Didn't you see how Oolie behaved when she thought you might be one? And she was so disappointed when you said she'd made a mistake. And . . ." The sneezing grew to a crescendo. "And when I called you 'Trueheart,' she went hurrying off the other way—and I'm sure it was to tell the troll king, and it'll be my fault if they send that huge mountain of a Mullius to catch you . . . and nobody can ever, ever, EVER stop him!"

Gracie forgot her fears at the sight of Flo's evident distress. She shook her head and smiled at the exhausted little bat. "You didn't mean to give me away," she said gently, "and I'm sure we can get out somehow." She paused to think. "If you go down that side tunnel, can you get to the outside world? I'm sure I saw daylight."

Flo nodded. "It's not a very big opening, though. *You* might be able to wriggle through, but your friend won't fit."

"I don't think either of us could jump over the pit," Gracie said with a shudder. "But you could fly out, Flo. Do you think you could take a message? A message to Marlon? He'll know what to do."

"Marlon?" Flo looked shocked. "Me? Go to find Mr. Batster?"

"Please," Gracie said. "Please, dear Flo. He'll tell Marcus and the Ancient Crones, and then they'll tell him how we can escape."

She sounded so confident that Flo sneezed, shook her wings, and sat up. "I'll try—but what about you?"

"Gubble and I'll look after each other until you get back," Gracie told her.

"If you say so, Trueheart." Flo hesitated. "What's your name? Who shall I say?"

"Gracie. Gracie Gillypot."

"OK, Gracie Gillypot. See you soon!" Flo flipped her wings and zoomed up the narrow tunnel like a small, determined arrow. The candle flame flickered as she went, and Gubble grunted.

Gracie squeezed his hand. "Don't worry, Gubble. Flo'll find Marlon, and we'll be out of here in no time." The wisp of silver on his wrist caught her eye, and she pointed at it. "That's pretty."

Gubble nodded, pulled the thread free, and held it out to her. "Yours."

"Oh! Thank you!" Gracie wove the silver in and out of one of her braids and smiled as she saw it glitter in the candlelight. "It almost looks as if it came from the web. Where did you find it?"

Gubble didn't answer. He grunted again. "Hear steps."

As he spoke, Gracie realized she could hear them too. They were still some ways away, but the ground beneath her feet was already beginning to shake.

"Do you know what, Gubble?" Gracie said, hoping her voice wasn't wobbling. "I think we'd better see if there's a way to get across that huge pit after all. I don't think I want to meet whatever it is that's coming, do you?"

Gubble said nothing. He had turned to inspect the tunnel wall behind him, pushing at the earth with his fingers. A moment later he was wrenching at a tree root as thick as Gracie's arm. A heavy shower of earth fell from the roof above, but Gubble shrugged it off and went on tugging.

"Gubble get in, Gubble get out," he muttered. "Get in, get out . . ."

Gracie bit her lip and made no comment. She knew from experience that when Gubble had that particular expression on his face, it was no use trying to stop him; even orders from the Ancient One herself had no effect when he was convinced that what he was doing was right.

"Ug." The tree root came away, setting off another avalanche.

Gracie looked up anxiously, wondering how far it was to the grass and the trees and the sunshine, and how many tons of rock and soil lay in between. Gubble began to attack another root, this one even more substantial. It felt to Gracie as if the whole tunnel was in imminent danger of collapse; she moved closer to Gubble, hoping his solid bulk would protect her.

"Ug, ug, UFF!" Gubble was pulling as hard as he could, his muscles bulging. His eyes were screwed shut, and every inch of him was concentrated on the root. He was covered in earth, and more was falling. A large lump of mud crashed down beside Gracie, sending the candle flying into darkness.

"Grind! Crush! Slay!" An echoing roar rolled down the tunnel toward them.

Gracie gave a terrified squeal and clutched at Gubble. Gubble grunted, gave a final mighty heave — and the tree root screamed and sprang back, dragging the troll and Gracie into a tiny confined space, where they were pressed together so tightly they could hardly breathe. The ground trembled as the heavy footsteps thundered nearer and nearer; Gracie shut her eyes and prayed that she and Gubble were invisible.

"TRUEHEART!" Mullius Gowk gave a wild bellow of triumph — but it was muffled by a massive fall of mud and rocks and earth. The enormous troll was buried, all but his feet.

Gracie was flung backward, and before she could catch her breath, she was seized by an irresistible force stronger than any wind. All she could think was, *I'm falling . . . falling UPWARD!* Up and up, up and up she whirled, until sunlight blinded her and she found herself tossed out of the darkness onto a patch of grass in front of an astonished Marlon, a dwarf, and a wide-eyed Alf. Behind her, a battered and broken birch tree limped hastily away to recover in the cool, dim depths of the Unreliable Forest.

There was no sign of Gubble.

Chapter Fourteen

Prince Vincent's mouth opened, shut, then opened again.

"Stupid boy!" his grandmother thundered. "You look like a cod!" She heaved an enormous sigh. "Are you a prince or a worm?"

Vincent's teeth began to chatter. "P-p-please, Grandmother, I'd rather be a worm than go out of the Five Kingdoms."

Queen Bluebell of Wadingburn looked at her grandson with disgust. "The Dowager Duchess of Cockenzie Rood assures me that Marigold will hardly have crossed the border. You're not likely to meet anything more ferocious than a cow." Seeing Vincent's face grow even paler, she hastily added, "In a field, you silly boy. In a field."

Vincent shuffled his feet and played with the tassel

on his sword belt. There was no sword; sharp things made him nervous. "But Grandmother . . . couldn't Marcus go instead? He likes adventures. I don't."

"That young man's already having adventures of his own." Bluebell decided the time had come to play her trump card. "Of course, I was thinking of sending you in my best traveling coach."

Prince Vincent brightened a little. "With a coachman? A *big* coachman?"

"The biggest coachman we can find," his grandmother assured him. "And there'll be a picnic. Marigold won't have had anything to eat for hours and hours, and she looks to me like a girl who likes her puddings and pies."

Vincent brightened even more. "A picnic? Hmm. I see. Would I be able to choose what's in the picnic?"

His grandmother took a deep breath. "Yes, Vincent. You may go to the kitchens this very minute and order whatever you like. Hurry up about it, though — I want you on your way as soon as possible."

Her grandson positively danced his way out of the schoolroom, and Bluebell sank into an armchair.

"Heavens to Betsy," she said as she fanned herself cool again. "What am I to do with the boy?"

Professor Scallio, part-time tutor to Prince Vincent

and his sister, Princess Loobly, looked up from a heavy leather-bound history book and suggested, "Find him a strong-minded princess. When he's older, of course."

"But who'd have him?" Bluebell asked gloomily. "Besides, the Five Kingdoms don't produce strong-minded princesses. You must have noticed that, Professor. My beloved Loobly hardly has a mind at all—although one hopes she'll be better when she's had a year or two of your excellent tuition."

The professor chuckled. "I must admit I was surprised to hear you say Princess Marigold had gone on an adventure."

"Hmph." The old queen put her feet up on Vincent's desk. "She's only gone because she's chasing after young Marcus, and he's gone hunting dwarves, or so Hortense tells me. Now, there's a lad with a bit of spirit."

"Indeed." Professor Scallio nodded. "A tutor should never admit to favorites, but I do have a very soft spot for that young man." He paused and rubbed his nose thoughtfully. "Did you say he was hunting dwarves?"

"Watching them, I should have said." Bluebell waved a casual hand. "Gone with Gracie Gillypot. That's why Marigold's rushed off. Green-eyed jealousy, I'd say." She gave the professor a piercing glance. "What's up? You look worried."

The professor picked up his book, then put it down again. "Just a thought. Nothing more."

Queen Bluebell took her feet off the desk and leaned forward. "What kind of thought?"

"I was wondering about the dwarves," Professor Scallio said slowly. "It's that wedding at Dreghorn. There's never been one quite as grand, and the orders for gold must be unimaginable. They must be under a lot of pressure. Could be a bit of a mistake to go looking for them just now. Wish he'd asked me first."

"But dwarves are jolly little chaps, aren't they?" Bluebell was puzzled. "Can be grumpy if they're not paid on time, but no real harm in them."

"No. That's true." The professor tapped the book in front of him. "But history can tell you a lot. In times of stress the dwarves have been known to call upon the trolls for help, and trolls are a very different type of character."

Bluebell frowned. "Rubbish, my dear professor. Trolls were dealt with hundreds of years ago, after that High King fellow died. We've got laws now. Agreements. Charters. Creatures like that are well under control, you mark my words. Besides, isn't that twin sister of yours one of the Ancient Crones? Surely she'd know if anything were wrong. And little Gracie's

a Trueheart. She won't have any trouble with trolls."
She heaved herself to her feet. "No, no, no. Those children are safe as houses. Which reminds me—you'll have to excuse me while I get Vincent on his way. Fingers crossed that he gets there without having eaten the entire contents of the picnic basket." The queen gave the professor a worldly-wise nod and sailed out of the parlor to rout Vincent from the kitchens and send him on his adventure.

Professor Scallio went back to his history book, but he was unable to concentrate. "Trolls," he murmured to himself. "Truehearts. Now . . . what was that story about trolls and Truehearts?" He took another even older book from the shelves and began to flick through the pages. "Here we are . . . yes." He read a paragraph, then read it again. "Oh, dear. Oh, dear, oh, dear, oh, dear.

"When Trueheart's life is ended here,
the High King's heart will beat once more
and power come to those who reign.
A King of Kings will rule again.

"Shocking rhyme, and may not be true, of course, but that doesn't matter. If the trolls believe it, it's dangerous."

The professor jumped to his feet and began to walk back and forth. "I'd better send a warning. But then again, maybe the Ancient One knows all about it? Dear me, dear me. But better safe than sorry. I'll send a bat, just to be sure."

Professor Scallio scribbled a note on a small piece of parchment, then hurried out of the schoolroom and into the library. There he clicked his fingers, and a small bat winged her way down from a shadowy bookcase. "Hello, Prof," she said cheerfully. "What can I do for you?"

"Millie, dear—could you take a message to the House of the Ancient Crones?" The professor handed over the scrap of parchment. "I'm a little concerned about Gracie."

Millie, the youngest in Marlon's widespread family of messenger bats, flew an anxious circle. "Oh, no! I'd do anything for Miss Gracie. Does Dad know about it?"

The professor shook his head. "I haven't seen Marlon in a long while. If you bump into him on your way, tell him to make sure Gracie doesn't go near any trolls." Catching sight of Millie's anxious face, he added, "It may be nothing. Don't worry too much."

"I'm off this second, Prof," Millie told him, and she was gone.

Professor Scallio walked over to the open library window and watched her zigzag into the afternoon sunshine. As he turned back to his books, there was a rumbling on the carriageway below, and Queen Bluebell's most luxurious traveling coach came rolling into sight. There was no sign of Prince Vincent, but the professor could see a number of baskets and boxes packed inside the coach, so he presumed the prince was somewhere among them. He smiled when he saw the size of the coachman; Vincent's grandmother had been as good as her word. "Let's hope he enjoys adventuring," Professor Scallio said aloud to himself. "Although I think there's little hope of that. If only he were more like Prince Marcus."

Chapter Fifteen

Marigold had slept for much of the day and had been dreaming. It had started as a wonderful dream in which she and Marcus were walking hand in hand under the stars, but after a while it had turned nasty. Something was chasing them, and Marcus wasn't taking it nearly seriously enough. He kept clapping his hands and telling her to listen for the beat of the happy little feet as they hurried down the street—

Marigold screamed and sat up. Her dream did not go away, however. The sound of hurrying feet continued—until she realized it was not feet at all, but hooves. Galloping hooves.

"Marcus!" Marigold shrieked as she scrambled to her feet and waved her arms wildly. "I'm here! Come and save me!"

Glee saw her out of the corner of his eye, swerved, then slowed to a walk. He had been seriously spooked by his collision with Gubble, and his long gallop through the forest had been exhausting; he was delighted to see someone he knew. Whenever he had come across Marigold in the past, she had cooed over him and fed him sugar, and comfort was what he most wanted just now. He was disconcerted when Marigold looked at his empty saddle and began to cry; lowering his head, he nuzzled hopefully at the rosebuds on her dress, but she went on crying.

"Marcus has fallen off," she sobbed, "or he's been eaten by a monster, and I'll never see him again . . . Whatever shall I doooooo?"

The pony, having discovered that the rosebuds were not only inedible but distinctly unpleasant, moved an indignant step or two away. Neither Marcus nor Ger, his stable boy, ever cried over him, and he was contemplating making his own way back to Gorebreath when Marigold suddenly realized that she might be about to lose a second pony in one day and caught at his reins. She and Glee looked at each other in some perplexity, both wondering what should happen next. They were saved from making a decision by the sound of someone running; before Marigold had a chance to scream or prepare herself in any way, Marcus came panting down the track, his face scarlet and his hair standing on end.

This was not at all how Marigold had envisaged his arrival, and although she was pleased to see that he had not been eaten by a monster, she made a face.

"You're all hot and sweaty," she said, pouting.

At that precise moment Marigold was the last person in the entirety of the Five Kingdoms that Marcus expected to see; she was also the last person he wanted to see. He was worried about Gracie and had been devastated to find that Glee had vanished. He had seen the broken branches and other signs of struggle where Glee and Gubble had collided, and had convinced himself that the pony had been carried off by some fierce and terrible animal and would never be seen again. Relief made him crotchety. "What on earth are you doing here?" he demanded. "And what are you doing with my pony?"

Marigold had no intention of replying to such rude questions. She patted her hair and smoothed her skirts, then checked to see if Marcus had noticed how delightfully she was dressed. As she looked up at his mud-spattered face, she made a surprising discovery. "You've been crying." She sniffed. "I thought you *liked* adventures!"

Marcus was now furious. "What I like and don't like isn't any business of yours, Marigold." He all but snatched Glee's reins from her hand, and swung himself into the saddle. "As it happens I'm on the most important adventure of my entire life, and it was nearly wrecked by you stealing my pony, and . . ."

Marcus's voice died away as he suddenly realized what he was saying. And remembered what he was meant to be doing. He stared at Marigold for so long that she began to blush.

"It's all right, Marcus," she simpered. "I know I look terribly, terribly pretty. And I didn't take your pony, you know. He came running up the road, but when he saw me he stopped at once." She fluttered her eyelashes. "I expect he was wondering why I was here on my own."

Marcus made no reply but went on staring. Marigold smiled her sweetest smile and twirled around twice so that the full glory of Fedora's sky-blue dress could be seen to its best advantage. "Aren't *you* wondering why I'm here?" she prompted.

"No," Marcus said. "Not really."

Marigold tried another twirl, but the prince frowned. "Would you mind not doing that? It's making me dizzy, and I'm trying to think."

"That's all right." Marigold did some more eyelash-fluttering. "Just as long as you're thinking about me." She was delighted to see Marcus nod in reply; she had begun to think he wasn't really worth bothering with, but this was much more hopeful. She tilted her head to one side. "Guess what I'm doing! Go on — guess!" As there was no response, she went on, "I'm having an adventure! It was such fun, until my naughty pony ran away . . . but now you've come hurrying to rescue me. Darling Marcus! Wouldn't you like to kiss me?"

"*Kiss* you?" Marcus looked so horrified that all Marigold's romantic dreams died a sudden and dramatic death. "Why would I want to kiss you?"

Marigold scowled at him. "I was . . . I was joking, stupid. Can't you take a joke?" She folded her arms. "I suppose I'll have to let you give me a ride home, seeing as Fedora's — I mean, my pony ran away. And I want to go now."

Marcus slowly dismounted, his thoughts whirling. He had promised to find a princess to take back to the dwarves, and fate had neatly placed a princess in his path, but now that it actually came to asking her to pay a visit to a troll—even if only for the shortest of times—he could see what a difficult task he had set for himself. In his head he had been thinking of one of Marigold's sisters; Arabella, perhaps, or Araminta. They were both inclined to giggle whenever Marcus came anywhere near them, but they would do almost anything if they were promised a new ballgown or a new pair of gloves. But *Marigold?* Marcus groaned loudly.

"What's the matter with you?" Marigold snapped. "Thinking of your stupid Gracie Gillypot, I suppose. Where is she, by the way?"

"Actually," Marcus said through gritted teeth, "she's in trouble. She needs help. Not that you'd care."

Marigold tossed her head. "I don't." This wasn't entirely true, but Marigold had no intention of showing that she was interested in such an ordinary girl. She was about to repeat her demand to be taken home when something small and dark and fluttery flew past, doubled back, and landed on Marcus's arm.

Marigold shrieked at the top of her voice; Marcus looked down and began to smile.

"Agh! Get it away from me! It's a bat!" Marigold's screams were piercing. "It'll get in my hair! It'll suck my blood! It's horrible!" She clutched at her head and ran to hide behind a tree.

"Hi, Millie," Marcus said. "How are you doing?"

Millie skittered up and down his wrist. "Very well, thank you, Mr. Prince. I don't suppose you've seen Dad anywhere, have you? Or Miss Gracie? The professor's worried about her, and he's sent me to the Ancient Crones with a warning."

Marcus's pulse began to race. "What kind of warning?"

"Trolls." Millie pulled the piece of parchment from under her wing and handed it over. "He looked ever so upset about it."

It took Marcus a moment to steady himself sufficiently to read the professor's minute, scholarly handwriting. "Trolls . . . Truehearts . . . High Kings . . ." he murmured. "What? I don't understand. They couldn't really do anything dreadful to Gracie, could they? I mean, Gubble's a troll, and he's her friend." A memory of the huge head that had appeared from the dwarves' earthworks came into his mind, but he shrugged away the notion that it could be dangerous. After all, it had been entirely under the control of Master Amplethumb, and Marlon had made no comment about there being any risks involved. And Gracie was a Trueheart; surely that protected her from evil and wickedness. No, Marcus decided, Professor Scallio must have gotten his facts muddled. He gave the parchment back to Millie. "You'd better take it to the Ancient Crones if the prof told you to," he said, "but I don't think we need worry too much about High Kings, or whatever they're called. I saw one of the underground trolls. He was absolutely enormous but about as clever as a brick. And I'm on a mission to make sure Gracie's OK. She fell into some kind of hole, but the dwarves promised they'd get her out, and I've promised to sort out everything else."

Marcus sounded slightly pleased with himself, and Millie gave him a sideways look as she put the message safely away. "If you say so, Mr. Prince. But I do sometimes wonder what goes on in those deep underground caverns. My mum used to scare me silly with stories when I was little. 'You'll be bat pie for a troll's dinner if you don't do as you're told!' she'd say." Marcus chuckled, and Millie stretched her wings. "I'd best be going. If you do see Dad, tell him to warn Miss Gracie."

As Millie departed, Marigold came out from behind her tree. "You're weird, Marcus," she said accusingly. "Really weird. If I'd known you talked to bats, I'd never have bothered with you. Now, are you going to take me home, or what?"

Marcus ran his hands through his hair, leaving it even wilder than before. Despite his brave assurances to Millie, he had no idea what to do next. "Take you home? I suppose I could," he said ungraciously. "That is—" He took a deep breath as desperation drove him to try an outside chance. "I don't suppose you'd like to come on an adventure? A *real* one?"

Marigold opened her mouth to say that she wouldn't go on an adventure with Marcus even if untold riches, heaps of pretty frocks, and a truly handsome prince were waiting at the other end, but a thought struck her and she was silent. Putting her finger in her mouth, she considered the proposition. She was, after all, dressed in the most exquisite dress in the whole wide world, and it would be a shame to waste it. She no longer had any romantic aspirations for Marcus's hand in marriage, but she was still piqued that he had chosen a pigtailed orphan as his companion . . . and wouldn't the pigtailed orphan be extremely taken aback, upset, and jealous to hear that Marigold had taken her place? "What kind of an adventure?"

Marcus, who had been certain Marigold would refuse, gathered his wits together as best he could. "Erm . . . there's a friend of mine . . . well, more a friend of a friend . . . and he wants to meet a princess." Inspiration struck. "He wants to meet a really *pretty* princess. And he'd like her to . . . to come to tea." It occurred to Marcus that he had no idea what trolls ate, but he remembered Gubble's activities of the morning. "There'll be chocolate cake, I expect."

"Will I get something nice if I come?" Marigold wanted to know. "Like treasure, or something?"

This was almost too much for Marcus, but he swallowed hard and kept a smile pinned to his face. "Of course you will." He mentally reviewed the contents of the ancient piggy bank that was lying somewhere at the bottom of a cupboard. "You can have anything you want. Well, almost."

Marigold fixed him with a gimlet eye. "What do you mean, 'almost'?"

"Why don't we get going?" Marcus suggested, with a degree of cunning he had never known he possessed. "And you can tell me all the things you want as we go."

"All right." Aware that she now had Marcus at a useful disadvantage, Marigold began to smile. "And I want to ride your—Oh! What's that?"

Both Marigold and Marcus swung around as a

large and opulent traveling coach came rattling down the track. On seeing Marigold, the coachman gave a loud whistle and pulled on the reins, and the four white horses came to a halt. The door opened, and Prince Vincent of Wadingburn stepped out.

"Princess Marigold," he announced with a grandiloquent bow, quite unaware of the jam liberally spread around his mouth, "I have come to rescue you from your adventure and take you safely home."

Marigold, delighted to be the object of such attention, curtsied. "Thank you, Vincent," she said. "But would you mind waiting a little while? I've got to go on an adventure with Marcus—but I won't be long, and it would be simply lovely to go home in a coach afterward."

"Oh." Vincent frowned. His instructions from his grandmother had been to drive to the border of the Five Kingdoms, collect Marigold, and bring her home again. "Can't you come straightaway? I've got a splendid picnic for us to share."

Marigold dithered. She had provided herself with a basket of sweets and cookies before leaving the palace, but the basket had gone off with Fedora's pony and cart and she was hungry. "I know!" she said. "You can come too, and we'll ride in your coach and eat our picnic as we go." She gave Marcus a cool glance. "Marcus can lead the way on his pony—can't you, Marcus?"

It was Vincent's turn to dither. "I don't know. Which way would we be going?"

Marigold looked at Marcus, and Marcus said, "That way." He pointed up the rough and stony track. "We're going to Flailing."

"No." Vincent shook his head. "No, no, no, no, no. That's not safe. We couldn't possibly." He turned to the coachman for support. "Grandmother would never allow it, would she, Fingle?"

The coachman, who had been chosen for his substantial bulk and muscle rather than his intelligence, shrugged his massive shoulders. "I couldn't say, Your Highness."

"There you are." Marigold took control of the situation. "Your grandmother won't mind at all, Vincent. Don't be so feeble. It'll be much more fun if we all go. Hurry up and get in the coach. Coachman, drive on!"

Chapter Sixteen

After she sat up, wiped the dirt out of her eyes, and smiled at Marlon and Alf, the first question Gracie asked was, "Where's Marcus?"

"He's gone to find a princess," Alf squeaked.

"A princess?" A chill gripped Gracie's stomach.

"It's a swap, see. He gets a princess for—"

"Alf!" Marlon cut his nephew short. He had noticed Gracie's bleak expression, and the tender heart that beat under his cool exterior would not allow him to leave her under any misapprehension. "It's a deal, kiddo. Nothing more. We wanted you dug out, and Bestius here agreed to do the deed, but he needs a princess for . . ." Marlon decided details were inappropriate. "We promised him a princess in exchange. The kid's gone riding off to find one. Be back soon."

"Oh." The chill lifted, and Gracie's thoughts went straight back to Gubble. "Marlon, you've got to help me! I must find Gubble. We were in a tunnel—it was really scary—and he found a way out for me, but somehow he got left behind."

Alf waved a cheery wing. "You don't want to go back down there, Miss Gracie."

"But I have to," Gracie said. "I absolutely *have* to." She looked pleadingly at Marlon.

"Alf's right. You've only just gotten out, kiddo," the bat protested. He had been delighted to see Gracie safe and sound, if covered in mud, and was distressed by her insistence on going back for Gubble. "I tell you—if *you* got out, the troll can too."

"What if he can't?" said Gracie, tears in her eyes. "I'd never forgive myself. No, I've got to find out what happened to him. Something huge was coming after us. I only got away because Gubble was so strong . . . but he didn't come with me." She fished in her pocket for a hankie and blew her nose hard. "I'm not going to cry about him. I'm going to find him."

"Yeah!" Alf squeaked. "Miss Gracie to the rescue!"

Marlon suppressed his nephew with a quelling glare and tried another approach. "What about the crones? Shouldn't you check with them?"

"And leave Gubble on his own? Never!" Gracie frowned.

Marlon sighed. "You're the truest of Truehearts, kid," he said. "OK. Where's the entrance to this tunnel of yours? The tree's hopped it."

It hadn't occurred to Gracie that there would be any difficulty in finding the tunnel entrance, and she looked around, perplexed. "It can't be far. Don't you know about it, Mr. Dwarf?"

Bestius shook his head. "Sorry, miss. Sounds like that was a troll tunnel, and we don't concern ourselves with those. There's only one we share, and we usually leave it well alone unless we have business with them."

"Couldn't I go down that?" Gracie asked, but she didn't wait for an answer. Seeing a small bat flitting between the trees, she leaped to her feet, waving her arms. "Flo! Flo? Is that you? I'm over here!"

Flo swooped down, saw Marlon and Alf, and was seized with such a paroxysm of sneezing that she landed flat on her back by Gracie's feet. Gracie picked her up and tried to calm her, but it was a couple of minutes before the little bat was able to speak.

"Wow! Some sneezing fit!" Alf was impressed. "Have you got hay—"

"Yes, she has," Gracie said quickly. "Flo, dearest

Flo, I haven't got time to explain, but please, please, *please* will you show me the way back into the tunnel? I've got to find Gubble. And as soon as you've shown me where to go, Alf'll take you to the Ancient Crones, and they'll make you better. You'll do that for me, won't you, Alf?"

"I'd do anything for you, Miss Gracie," Alf declared, "but if you're going into a tunnel, then I'm coming too."

"Cut the heroics, kid." Marlon eyed his nephew with exasperated affection. "You do as you're told. *I'm* going with Gracie. Which way, young Flo?"

Seeing Flo was about to be overcome again, Gracie said, "Quick! Point, Flo—point with your wing!" She looked over her shoulder at Bestius. "Are there any planks nearby? Or even a ladder? There's a simply enormous pit in the tunnel floor and there's no way I can get around it. I'll need to crawl over . . ."

The dwarf's face cleared, and he nodded. "Back in a sec." He hurried off.

Gracie, Marlon, and Alf followed the speechless Flo's waved instructions. It was a short walk to a small mound covered in briars and bracken; the entrance to the tunnel was neatly concealed behind a fallen pine tree, its roots bare and pointing to the sky.

A moment later, Bestius appeared, carrying a sturdy ladder and a spade; his eyebrows rose as he joined Gracie and her party of bats. "Well, I never! Fancy me not knowing there was an entrance here. The Old Trolls used to have secret spy-holes and tunnels all over this forest, but I thought they'd been sealed up for safety's sake." He pulled at his beard thoughtfully and crooked a finger at Marlon. "Excuse me for asking," he said in a low voice, "but this doesn't alter our agreement, does it? I mean, the young lady got out safe and sound without our help, and now she's going underground again of her own free will. The prince won't hold it against us, will he? He'll still bring us a princess?"

Marlon blinked as he realized that things were beginning to get complicated, but, being a bat with a strong belief in his ability to survive any crisis, he merely said, "No worries. The kid'll come good."

Gracie was studying the ladder. "I think it'll be long enough; I just hope I can get it through the entrance."

Bestius tipped his hat to her. "It would be my pleasure to help you, miss." He swung his spade, and in seconds the tunnel entrance had doubled in size. Gracie smiled at him, her eyes shining. "Oh, that's wonderful! Even Gubble will be able to get out now. Thank you so much."

"Stand back, kiddo." Marlon flew over her shoulder. "I'll check it out." Alf flew straight after him; there were sounds of argument and protestation — and then a long silence.

Gracie, clutching the ladder, strained her ears but could hear nothing. She turned to Flo, but the little bat had no answers.

"I can't hear any more than you can," she apologized. "It's all the sneezing. My ears get blocked. I'll go and see what they're up to." With a flick of her wings, she too was gone, and Gracie was left waiting restlessly for one or all of them to return.

"You don't think something could be catching them, do you?" she asked Bestius.

He shook his head. "They've gone exploring, I'd say. Looking for that friend of yours. What was his name? Gubble? Another prince, is he? That Prince Marcus was properly upset when he thought you were stuck underground. All in a tizzy, he was, make no mistake."

Gracie concealed her pleasure at this information with a laugh. "Gubble's a troll," she explained. "He lives with me at the House of the Ancient Crones."

Bestius gulped. "The . . . crones? The ones who spin the web? The web of power?"

"That's right." Gracie nodded. "Do you know them?"

The dwarf gulped again. He had convinced himself that it was allowable to hide a few unpalatable facts about trolls from Marcus, but this information made him look at things from a very different perspective. If word ever got back to the Ancient One that a dwarf had had anything to do with leading a friend of theirs—or even the friend of a friend of theirs—into danger, then anything might happen. Bestius began to chew the end of his beard while he tried to think what he should say.

Before he could say anything, Marlon, Alf, and Flo came flying out of the tunnel bursting with news. "He's there, Miss Gracie!" Alf did a double spin in his excitement. "Gubble's there, but he's got a tree root wrapped around him, so he can't get out, and *loads* of earth have come down! And there's the most enormous pair of feet you ever did see sticking out from underneath, and I wanted to tickle them but Unc said not to!" Alf ended his breathless report with another spin and a double dive before settling on a twig close beside Gracie. Flo settled next to him and confirmed his report with several sneezes.

"It's cool, kiddo." Marlon stretched his wings. "Checked the pit too—you'll be OK if you take it steady on the ladder. Watch the troll doesn't shift it on the way back—he's heavier than you."

Gracie nodded. "Will you come with me? It gets really dark in the main tunnel."

Bestius, who was feeling more and more guilty, reached into his coat pocket and produced the lantern he used when working. He lit it with his tinderbox and handed it to Gracie. "Here, miss." Gracie's beaming smile did not improve the way he was feeling, and he added, "I'll come after you and hold the ladder steady while you crawl across."

"Thank you," said Gracie. "You're very kind."

Bestius felt even worse. As Gracie crawled into the tunnel, he was so deep in thought that she had already dragged the ladder into place over the pit and was almost halfway across before he realized what she was doing. He hurriedly scrambled after her and held the ladder safely in position until she reached the other side.

"It's OK," Gracie called over her shoulder. "You can let go now."

The dwarf looked down at the ladder, then beyond into the darkness of the tunnel, where the glow of

Gracie's lamp was steadily getting smaller and smaller. "Oh, oddspillikins," he said, and slapped himself on the chest. "Bestius Bonnyrigg, are you a dwarf or a sneaky, sniveling goblin?" And he set off after Gracie.

Marlon, who had been watching the dwarf with interest, chuckled to himself. "Typical Trueheart, our Gracie. Brings out the best in the good, and the worst in the bad." He called for Alf and Flo, but there was no sign of them. The two little bats had vanished. Marlon called again with increasing irritation. Finally he heard a series of distant answering squeaks — but it was not Alf or Flo who flew down to join him.

It was his daughter, Millie, and she was looking ruffled. "Dad! Have you seen Miss Gracie? There's an urgent message from Miss Val's brother. Miss Gracie's not to go near any trolls — well, not meaning Gubble, of course, but any other ones. If you see her, can you tell her? I'm off to the House — the professor said they might know anyway, but I've got to make sure."

"Hang around, kid," her father said as Millie showed signs of flying off again. "What's the panic?"

Millie paused. "I've got one of my feelings, Dad. Mr. Prince says it's all OK, but —"

Marlon held up an imperative claw. "You've seen the Royal? Where? What was he doing?"

"I don't know," Millie said peevishly. "He was with a girl; she was hiding behind a tree, but I saw her. All in flounces and petticoats, but nothing like as nice as Miss Gracie. And Mr. Prince said Miss Gracie had fallen in a hole but not to worry—but I AM worried, Dad, and we've got to find her!"

Marlon put a comforting wing around his agitated daughter. "It's cool, kiddo. Young Gracie's safe as houses down that tunnel. Gubble's in trouble, but she'll save him." Marlon's tone was admiring. "Sounds as if the Royal's doing good too. Found a dame already, I'd say." He puffed out his chest. "It's a plan, Millie my girl. Going like clockwork."

Millie refused to be impressed. "Do Miss Val and Miss Edna and Miss Elsie know about it?"

"The crones? Natch."

Marlon had only hesitated for a fraction of a second before replying, but it was enough for Millie. "You haven't told them, have you? Not all of it, anyway. I know you, Dad—you think you can sort everything out all by yourself, and I know you're wonderful and as clever as can be, but this is serious stuff. Like I said, I've got a feeling. A bad one."

Marlon gave his only daughter a loving nibble on her ear. "Old worryguts. OK. Here's the deal.

Gracie'll be in and out of that tunnel in a couple of ticks, and she'll bring the troll with her. Young Marcus is collecting a princess—guess it's the dame you saw. She'll be delivered to the dwarves, 'n' the dwarves'll take her to the troll king. Then she gets rescued by Marcus with trumpets and stuff, and the kid's a hero. Check!" Marlon finished with a flourish and waited for the applause.

None came. Instead there was a thoughtful silence until Millie said, "I don't get it. Why does the princess have to go and see the troll king in the first place?"

Marlon was beginning to sense that his plan was not being as well received as he had hoped. "The dame's by way of a swap. But there's no need to bother your—"

Millie was in the air, raging. "Dad! Don't you DARE! I'm going straight to Miss Edna, and I want you to promise you'll stop Mr. Prince this minute! The very idea! That princess may be nothing but frills and fancy clothes, but she's still a girl, and girls have feelings, and you're treating her just like a . . . like a PARCEL! I never, ever thought I'd say this, but I'm ashamed of you, Dad—I really am." And Millie gave a heartbroken sob as she flew swiftly away.

A deflated Marlon watched her go. He was genuinely taken aback by her outburst; part of him was worried because he had upset her, but another part wondered if his plan could, in fact, be altered without the most terrible consequences. Coming to the conclusion that it would be impossible, he began to justify his actions. "Little Millie don't know the whole story—that's the problem. We only got the royal dame involved because we wanted young Gracie dug out. Couldn't have known she'd pop up like a bunny from a hole, could we?" He shifted from foot to foot as he waited for the uncomfortable knot in his stomach to subside. It didn't, and he began to feel angry instead. "Too independent, that young bat. Hmph. Needs to mind her own business!" And he shot into the tunnel to check on Gracie.

He was traveling at such a speed that he was quite unable to avoid Bestius, who was carefully maneuvering himself off the ladder at the far end. As Marlon thudded into the back of his head, Bestius yelped in surprise before rolling onto solid ground. The ladder slid sideways, wobbled, then fell down, down, and down again into the murky depths of the pit.

Chapter Seventeen

Queen Bluebell was feeling extremely pleased with her success in sending Prince Vincent on a mission to rescue Marigold. It seemed to her it had all the right ingredients: not too much danger and possibly even the beginnings of a useful romance. She was comfortably settled in her favorite armchair drinking a large, self-congratulatory glass of something considerably stronger than tea when the Dowager Duchess of Cockenzie Rood was announced.

"Hortense!" Bluebell said in surprise. "I thought you'd be helping soothe Kesta's ruffled feathers!" She shook her head. "Kesta's a good woman, but she does get herself into a terrible state about those girls of hers. Have a glass of Wadingburn's Best Old Malt. Excellent stuff."

The duchess shook her head. "That's kind of you, but not just now. I've come to ask your advice."

"Advice?" The queen raised an eyebrow. "What sort of advice?"

Hortense sat down on the edge of a sofa. "I've been wondering if I should go after Marigold." She saw Bluebell's eyebrow rise even higher and hastily added, "I know you've sent Vincent to rescue her, and it's a splendid plan if it works—but I can't help worrying. I never expected her to help herself to Fedora's dress and her pony and cart, and if she's surprised me once, she might surprise me again. What if the silly girl hasn't stopped at the border of the Five Kingdoms? What if she's gone chasing into the Enchanted Forests to find Marcus? He was off to Flailing to look at the dwarves." She paused and looked guilty. "That's what I told her to do. I haven't told Kesta, though."

"Hmph." Bluebell frowned. "I see your point. Vincent's far too chicken to go looking for her if she's not where she's meant to be."

"I feel so responsible." The dowager duchess sighed. "I thought it would do her good to have an adventure. I should have realized that she doesn't have the sense to do it properly. Do you think she'll come to any harm if she *has* gone to Flailing? She's wearing her sister's wedding dress, so she's not exactly hiding the fact that she's a royal princess. Stupid girl. You and I used to borrow the milkmaids' dresses, and nobody looked at us twice."

Her friend took her feet off her footstool, sat up, and rang the large bell on the floor beside her. When a small page appeared, Bluebell said, "Be a chum and fetch the professor for me." The boy shot off, and the queen turned to Hortense. "We'll ask Scallio what he thinks about it all. Good chap, even if he can't do a thing with Vincent. His sister lives in the More Enchanted Forest, and she tells him things I know nothing about. Gets a bit excited, sometimes — was wittering on about trolls earlier, and we all know they're no trouble these days — but overall he talks a lot of sense."

The duchess nodded and sat back among the sofa cushions.

A moment later, Professor Scallio appeared, a large book tucked under his arm; Queen Bluebell waved for him to join them. "Need your help," she said. "This adventure I told you about — Princess Marigold. What if she goes as far as Flailing? Any danger, would you say?" She paused. "Girl's all dressed up in her sister's wedding dress."

If Professor Scallio was in any way taken aback by this information, he did not show it. He stroked his chin while he considered what to say. His first thought

was that this could be an excellent opportunity to make sure Marcus and Gracie were safe, but he was a man of honor and not prepared to take advantage of his employer. "Well," he said slowly, "am I right in supposing she has a pony and cart?"

Bluebell and Hortense nodded.

The professor went on thinking. "The roads are decidedly rough beyond the border, so traveling is not always easy, and the different tracks—such as they are—have no signposts. I would suspect the princess might well give up long before she reaches the Unreliable Forest, which is where there might perhaps be some"—he coughed—"some uncertainty."

Bluebell gave him a hard stare. "Is that meant to be a joke?"

"Certainly not, Your Majesty." The professor looked shocked at the idea.

Hortense leaned forward. "That—what did you call it? Unreliable Forest. Sounds nasty. Should we call out the army, do you think?"

"Oh, no, ma'am." Professor Scallio's tone was definitive. "There are a number of treaties and truces in place that mean the armies of the Five Kingdoms can cross the border only in an extreme emergency.

There are some who would consider a military presence beyond the border to be a declaration of war."

There was a loud and cheery snort from Bluebell as she banged the duchess on the back. "Well done, Hortense! There's a thought! All-out war! Distract us nicely from Fedora's wedding, and you can't tell me that wouldn't be a blessed relief."

Professor Scallio smiled but shook his head. "I'm sure it won't come to that, Your Majesty. If I might make a suggestion, perhaps I could look for the princess myself? I have the advantage of knowing the forests well." He did not add that he also had the confidence of a number of highly intelligent bats who would be invaluable in the search for the lost princess.

Both Queen Bluebell and the duchess looked at him with undisguised relief. "Splendid!" Bluebell told him. "Excellent idea. Take any horse you want. Any carriage."

The professor bowed. "Thank you, Your Majesty. And if I find all is well and your grandson has found the princess and is happily escorting her home, I will not interfere." There was a twinkle in his eye as he added, "Neither will I inform him that I am . . . shall we say, the reserve rescue mission." He bowed once more and left the room.

"There." Bluebell reached for her glass. "Problem solved. Was almost expecting you to say you'd go with him, Hortense."

The duchess smiled. "I did think of it—but I'd better go back and try to keep Kesta calm. At least I can reassure her that everything's under control and there's a responsible adult on his way to look for Marigold." She reached for a glass. "Thank you. Thank you very much."

The queen laughed and filled Hortense's glass to the rim. "Here's to secondhand adventures. Cheers!"

Chapter Eighteen

Marcus was not happy. His idea of being a hero did not include riding slowly in front of a laboring coach, especially when the occupants were very obviously enjoying a substantial and delicious picnic from which he was excluded. Nothing had come his way other than a couple of cheese sandwiches and an overcooked sausage. It sounded as if Marigold and Vincent were getting along extremely well; Marcus was far too modest to guess that Marigold's shrieks of girlish enthusiasm were designed to make him go green with jealousy and realize how foolish he was to prefer a mere orphan to a princess.

Vincent, who, when his grandmother was elsewhere, was inclined to regard himself as something of a beau, was delighted by Marigold's smiles and laughter. He managed two quite reasonable jokes and began to think she was the prettiest princess he had ever seen; this pleased Marigold even more, and she asked if he would like her to sing him a song. "Go for it," Vincent told her. "Although I'm not very good at singing myself. Can't tell 'Pop Goes the Star' from 'Twinkle, Twinkle, Little Weasel.'"

Marigold gave him a forgiving smile and began to sing. The coachman woke up with a jolt, and the horses broke into a trot. Glee's ears flickered, and Marcus winced as he rode as far ahead as he dared.

Vincent, completely unaware of the sudden increase in speed, gazed at Marigold. "That's amazing," he breathed. "You sing like . . . like . . . nothing I've ever heard before. It's SO amazing. Are you going to sing at the wedding?"

This possibility had already occurred to Marigold, but her suggestion had been firmly quashed by Fedora. Even Queen Kesta had failed to support her, and the refusal had rankled. Now, it seemed, she had found an ally. She fluttered her eyelashes. "Dear Vincent—do you think I should? Truly?"

Vincent nodded enthusiastically. "I've never heard anyone sing the way you do. It made the hairs stand up on the back of my neck. You're . . . you're *amazing*, Marigold."

Marigold's heart beat faster. If Vincent had been just a little taller, she would have kissed him, but she did not hold his size against him. He would grow, and she could wait. In the meantime, she could use him for other purposes. "Vincent," she whispered, "will you walk with me in the wedding procession?"

Vincent stared at her. "But you're walking with Marcus."

"I'll tell Mother I don't want to. I want to walk with you." Marigold squeezed his arm. "You'd like that, wouldn't you? And when we get to the cathedral steps, we can stop in front of Fedora and Tertius, and I can sing a song to them while you make sure nobody interrupts." Marigold did not think it necessary to say that she had already put this plan to Marcus, and he had laughed so much he had gotten the hiccups.

Vincent's eyes grew wide. "Wow, Marigold! You'd really sing to them in front of everybody? What an amazing girl you are!"

Marigold looked smug. "I am, aren't I? So it's all settled, then? You'll walk with me, and we'll keep our surprise a secret just between us two."

Nobody had ever asked Vincent to keep a secret before. Nor had a beautiful princess with golden curls and big blue eyes ever fluttered her eyelashes at him. He gulped, coughed, blew his nose, tucked his handkerchief back in his pocket, and took Marigold's hand. "Marigold," he said hoarsely, "I'd do anything for you. Absolutely anything. You're the most amazing girl I've ever met, and I'll keep your secret forever and ever and ever."

"Not forever, darling," Marigold said with another flutter of her eyelashes. "Just until the wedding. And now that I see you *do* have a hankie, perhaps you could use it to wipe the jam off your face?" She sweetened this request by giving him her most charming smile, and Vincent's capture was complete.

Marigold celebrated her success by peeping out of the coach window; she was horrified to see that they were deep in the middle of a forest of tall and twisted trees, with branches pointing menacingly at her. She let out a shriek, and Vincent hurried to her side. He shrieked too, and they clutched each other like two babes in the wood.

"Stop the coach! Stop this minute! Where are we? Stop! Stop, I say!"

The coach lumbered to a halt, and Marcus rode back to see what was the matter. Two indignant faces glared at him.

"We don't want to be here!" Marigold said in her most imperious tones. "And I've changed my mind. I don't want to go on an adventure with you. We want to go home, don't we, Vincent darling?"

Vincent nodded. "We certainly do."

Marcus sighed. "Don't you want any chocolate cake?"

Marigold, who had been eating cake nonstop for the past couple of hours, shook her head. "What kind of baby do you think I am? Fingle, turn the coach around this minute!"

Fingle looked to the left and mumbled something under his breath. He looked to the right and mumbled again.

"What's he saying?" Vincent demanded.

"I think," Marcus said, trying not to sound too pleased, "he's saying he can't. There isn't room. We'll have to go a bit farther to find a turning place."

The two heads disappeared, and there was a lot of loud whispering before the door opened and Vincent got out, looking self-important. "I'm checking for myself," he announced. But he soon saw there was no option other than to continue. The trees grew thick on either side; there was only just room for the coach to move forward. Vincent held up a commanding hand. "Turn the coach around just as soon as you can," he ordered. The coach-man nodded, and Vincent climbed back inside. "We'll soon be home," he reported. "There's sure to be a turn-ing place. Why don't you sing me another song?"

Marigold, who had never ever been asked to sing a second song by anyone who had heard the first, began to feel a genuine fondness for the stout little prince. "Darling Vincent," she cooed, "of course I will."

As the tuneless wailing began once more, Marcus groaned and encouraged a more-than-willing Glee to increase the distance between him and the coach. From close by, a familiar voice squeaked, "Hello, Mr. Prince! What's that noise?"

"Alf!" Marcus slowed his pony and grinned. "It's Princess Marigold. She's singing to Vincent, and he actually likes it!"

Alf looked pained. "Hurts my ears. What do you think, Flo?"

Another bat, much the same size as Alf, came wing-ing toward Marcus, then stopped to perch on a twig. She began to speak but was overcome with a fit of sneezing so violent that she was unable to continue.

"Hay fever," Alf explained. "Miss Gracie says she'll get it cured for her."

"Have you seen Gracie?" Marcus asked eagerly.

"Have the dwarves dug her out? Is she OK?"

Alf nodded. "Gone down a tunnel to rescue Gubble. Uncle Marlon's there too. And a dwarf. Me and Flo are on our way to the crones, but Flo's never been out of the tunnels, so I was showing her around a bit—and then we saw you." Alf twirled in a circle around Marcus's head. "Never met a prince before, have you, Flo?"

There was another explosion of sneezing, which Marcus ignored. "What do you mean, she's 'down a tunnel'?" His voice sharpened. "What kind of tunnel? And why's Gubble stuck? Where did he come from?"

Alf, delighted to impress Flo with his familiarity with royalty, settled himself on Glee's saddle and made a full report. He finished by describing the enormous feet sticking out from the pile of earth from the tunnel roof, and Marcus looked thoughtful. "I expect that's the huge troll I saw in the clearing. He didn't look very clever; maybe he brought the roof down by mistake."

"Unc wouldn't let me tickle his toes," Alf told him. "Said it might wake him up."

"I wish I'd been there to help," Marcus said. "Gracie always has better adventures than me."

He sounded as if he thought Gracie had been having

fun, and Flo took a deep breath. "She's very brave, Gracie Gillypot is." She forgot her fears in her desire to defend Gracie and landed on Marcus's arm. "When that horrid Oolie had hold of her and was dragging her to the king, she never screamed—"

"*What?*" Marcus sat bolt upright and stared at the tiny bat. "What are you talking about? What king?"

Flo, unnerved, went into a fit of sneezing.

Marcus looked at Alf, but Alf looked blank. "Miss Gracie didn't say anything about kings. All she said was she wanted to rescue Gubble . . ."

Marcus turned back to Flo. "Please," he said, "please try to tell me."

Struggling between nerves and sneezes, Flo did her best to explain. "Trueheart!" she gasped. "Trolls! Oolie . . . BAD. Oolie . . . danger . . ." It was too much for her, and she collapsed in a heap.

Marcus picked her up as gently as he could, but she showed no signs of recovery. "What's the matter with her?" he asked Alf. Alf shook his head helplessly, and Marcus, after a moment's consideration, slipped Flo into his pocket. He was beginning to feel seriously concerned. The desperation in Flo's words had cut through his romantic dreams of heroic deeds and brought him back to reality with a bump. "We need to find Gracie," he said. "And I want to find out what's really been going on. I've got a feeling it's not nearly as simple as Marlon made out."

"I'll show you where Miss Gracie is," Alf volunteered, and Marcus gave him a thumbs-up before swinging around and riding back to the coach.

"Marigold! Vincent!" he called. "I'm going to ride on ahead!"

Vincent's head popped out of the coach window. "You can't," he began — but Marigold appeared beside him.

"He can make himself useful and look for a turning place," she said. "Can't you, Marcus? And hurry up. It's getting late. We want to get home." She thumped the side of the coach to make her point. "I'm *so* not coming on any adventures with you again! Not EVER!"

Marcus, glad of the excuse and only too aware of how time was passing, waved agreement, but Marigold had seen Alf circling above his head. With a loud scream she pulled Vincent back inside and slammed the window shut. Marcus eased Glee into a canter and rode on.

Chapter Nineteen

The Ancient One was icing Gubble's chocolate cake when Millie came flitting through the window. "Hello, Millie," she said, her one blue eye twinkling—and then she saw Millie's face. "Oh, dear. Bad news?"

"It's not very good, Miss Edna." Millie shook her head. "The professor sent a message to remind you about some prophecy." She pulled the piece of parchment from under her wing and held it out. "Here."

Edna read it, then read it again. "'When Trueheart's life is ended here . . .'—oh, dearie, dearie me—'the High King's heart will beat once more . . .'—that sounds thoroughly unpleasant—'and power come to those who reign.' Hmm. No wonder the professor thinks the trolls will get excited. 'A King of Kings will rule again.' Well—that's obvious enough, and yes, it's really rather worrying. It's been so much quieter since the trolls agreed to sign the Charter of Peace—although I understand there were shady goings-on at the time and the new king wasn't, strictly speaking, the one who should have taken power. Hmph. Have you seen Gracie? Your father said she'd fallen down a troll trap. I suggested he ask the dwarves to help her."

Millie sighed. "I saw Prince Marcus, and he said she was down some hole but it was all OK; the dwarves were going to dig her out—but then I saw Dad, and he said Miss Gracie was crawling around in a tunnel, and I've got *such* a nasty feeling about it."

Edna did not say that the curious stains spreading across the web suggested that Millie might be right. Instead she asked, "What kind of tunnel?"

Millie shook her head. "I don't know, Miss Edna. But Dad . . . he's got one of his plans, and I don't like it at all. Something to do with a princess and a huge troll digging for the dwarves, and Mr. Prince was going to rescue the princess—and surely he should be looking out for Miss Gracie, not playing at being a hero!"

The Ancient One's round blue eye widened as she took in this new information. "Millie, dear," she said at last, "have you seen Gubble?"

"That's why Miss Gracie was going down the tunnel," Millie said. "He was stuck, Dad said, but he did say they'd be out in two ticks."

"I think I need to speak to Marlon."

There was a steely note in the Ancient One's voice, and as Millie fluttered up to the open window, she was wondering if she should have said as much as she had. "I'm sure he meant it for the best, Miss Edna."

"I'm sure he did," Edna said grimly. "And that's what's worrying me."

Chapter Twenty

Gracie had been too preoccupied with making her way down the dark and narrow tunnel to hear the ladder fall behind her. The first she knew of it was when Marlon appeared beside her, blinking in the light of the lamp.

"Bit of a mistake," he remarked. "Lost the ladder. Still, we've got the dwarf." He pointed behind him, and Gracie became aware of a steady muttering and grumbling coming toward them. About to ask how they were going to escape without a ladder, she was distracted by a faint groan.

"Gubble!" she said. "Gubble! Where are you?"

"Ug. Ug."

Gracie held the lamp up high. The flame shone out, showing a heap of earth in the center of the main tunnel. As Alf had reported, there were two large feet emerging; Gracie bit her lip as she thought she saw one foot move, but decided it was the unsteady light. Then she caught sight of Gubble and forgot everything else. He was pinned against the tunnel wall, a thick tangle of roots holding him so tightly he could hardly breathe. He was covered in mud, except for a wet trail of tears that trickled down his dirty green cheeks.

"*Poor* Gubble," Gracie said. As she bent over him, her braids swung forward, and the silver thread glittered and gleamed. Gubble gave a surprised grunt.

"Sorry." Gracie pushed her hair back impatiently, but as she did so, it was her turn to be surprised. The roots were shriveling in front of her eyes, and a moment later they were gone.

Gubble took several deep breaths, stepped forward, and swung his arms to and fro. "Nins and peedles," he explained. "Sore."

Marlon chuckled. "Power of Trueheart," he announced. "Good work, kiddo. Now, let's think how to get out." He flew a circle and looked inquiringly at Bestius, who was emerging, still muttering, from the side tunnel. "Any ideas?"

Bestius didn't answer. He was staring at the feet.

Gracie followed his gaze and put her hand over her mouth in horror. This time there was no doubt.

There was a twitch, then another, and the heap of earth shook as if suffering its own small volcanic eruption. From somewhere underneath came a deep and angry rumble.

"Mullius." Bestius breathed in. "Mullius Gowk." He glared at Marlon. "If you hadn't bumped into me, we'd be on our way back across the ladder; whereas now we're in trouble. *Big* trouble!"

Marlon sniffed. "Don't remember inviting you to join the party. Besides, I thought you were pally with these guys."

"Not this one." The dwarf shivered. "He used to eat us dwarves for breakfast. He's an Old Troll, with the old ways." He gave Marlon a sour look. "Very fond of bat pie."

"I think," Gracie said as calmly as she could, "this isn't quite the moment to worry about anything except how to get out of here." She stopped as the heap of earth moved again. "Oh! *Please* don't argue—we've got to get away NOW!"

Bestius nodded. His heart was beginning to beat uncomfortably fast at the thought of a furious Mullius. He slung his spade across his shoulder and took command. "We'll go down the tunnel. Follow me!" And he set off at a steady trot.

"Go," Gubble agreed, and Gracie took his hand as they hurried after the dwarf. A moment later there was a convulsive heaving and shuddering as the earth fell away from the enormous hairy bulk of the Old Troll; there was more angry rumbling, and he began to haul himself up to a sitting position.

"FASTER!" Bestius said urgently.

Gubble did his best to obey, but he was exhausted by his struggles to escape. Bestius, muttering anxiously under his breath, came back to take Gubble's arm. He and Gracie half lifted, half pulled the troll along between them, Marlon zigzagging beside Gracie.

"You're doing good, kiddo," he announced. "I'll check it out ahead. Trust your uncle Marlon."

"Marlon!" Gracie whispered, "I've had an idea! What if you take the lamp? Would it be too heavy for you? Only once that—that thing is properly on his feet, he'll catch us in no time, but if we could find somewhere to hide in the darkness, maybe you could lead him past."

Bestius nodded. "Good idea. It'd give me time to work out where to go."

Marlon did a fast dive. "Sharp as well as True," he said admiringly. "Let's try."

"Wait until we find somewhere to hide." Gracie was panting as she ran; Gubble was heavy, and half

his weight was on her arm. "Don't take the lamp until you have to. . . ."

"There's a bend ahead," Bestius said, puffing. "Once we're beyond that, it'll be easier to hide without him noticing."

There was no more talking as Gracie and the dwarf lugged Gubble for several more minutes. At last they had rounded the bend and began keeping an eye out for side tunnels or some sort of gap or recess, but there was none that they could see. Gracie was getting desperate; her legs felt like lead, and her arms and shoulders were aching. She forced herself to keep on running, even though every step was an effort.

"Ug." Gubble tugged at her arm.

"He's after us." Bestius sounded grim. "I can feel the ground shaking . . . although he's not coming that fast . . . not yet, anyway."

Gracie's stomach lurched as she squinted ahead, praying for a crack in the walls . . . anywhere they could hide.

"There!" Marlon swung in front of her, making the lamp flame quiver. "Over there, guys — see?"

Marlon was right. It was not much more than a narrow gap between two particularly thick and twisted tree roots, but it was better than anything they had seen up until then. Bestius dropped Gubble's arm and hurled himself toward it; a moment later he had disappeared. "Bigger than it looks from the outside," he reported in a muffled whisper.

This was optimistic; there was barely room for the three of them. Squeezing Gubble through dislodged a fair quantity of soil, but, as Marlon pointed out, their pursuer was making his way through the darkness and was unlikely to notice. "Let's try the lamp, kiddo," he said.

Gracie placed it around his neck, but he could fly only a short way before the weight became too much for him and he was forced to land.

"Can we make it lighter?" Gracie asked.

Bestius considered, pulling at the end of his beard. "We could pour out some of the oil. It's pretty full. That would lighten it—but the flame'll go out that much sooner."

Even the walls of their hiding place were starting to shake. Gracie swallowed hard before she said, "We have to try. I can't think of anything else to do."

Bestius took the lamp and all but emptied it. Marlon nodded approvingly as it was lit once more. "Stay here, you three," he ordered. "I'll fly just out of sight so all that monster sees is the glow. Once he's past, make your move." Gracie dropped a kiss on the top of his head, and he quivered in embarrassment. "No prob, kid. Keep cool," he muttered, and took off before she could kiss him again.

Bestius and Gracie watched as the lamplight zigzagged into the distance, leaving only a faint glow up ahead. A moment later they realized that the heavy footsteps were coming unpleasantly close, and they cowered back in their hiding place. The tree roots would give them no protection if they were discovered. Gracie froze as Mullius thudded nearer and nearer, snarling as he came.

"Grind. Crush. Slay. Blood. Guts. Kill."

Then he was beside them, and they could smell sweat and earth and hot breath that stank of rottenness and decay. Gracie clutched Gubble's hand so hard she felt him wince, but he made no sound. None of them dared move until Mullius Gowk was long past, thundering after the ever-retreating glow of the lamp.

"Phew," Bestius said at last as the sound of footsteps finally faded away and silence gradually surrounded them. "Let's give it a couple more minutes, shall we?

And maybe have a bite to eat. Still haven't eaten my lunch."

Gracie nodded, then remembered the dwarf couldn't see her. "Yes," she agreed. "That would be lovely." There were sounds of a bag being unpacked and the rustle of paper, then a slice of hard bread was pushed into her hand. Gracie, who was so hungry she would happily have eaten burned porridge, ate it gratefully and found it surprisingly filling.

Gubble ate his with noisy enthusiasm before slumping against Gracie's side. "Tired," he remarked. A moment later he began to snore.

Gracie and the dwarf sat without speaking until a sudden fall of earth from above made them jump. "What's that?" Gracie whispered as she shook dirt out of her hair. "Is that monster coming back?"

Bestius was listening intently. "I don't think so. But there's something going on. . . ."

Gracie strained her ears, but her hearing was not as acute as the dwarf's. "I can't hear anything. What is it?"

"Digging," said Bestius with a faint chuckle. "It's OK. If I've got my directions right, and I usually have, we're not that far from the Flailing road—and that means there's the biggest troll you've ever seen digging away somewhere nearby in one of our mines. There's a bit of a shake . . . Can you feel it?"

Gracie realized she could feel a vibration under her feet. It was faint but steady: *thud-thud-thud-thud-thud-thud-thud* . . . as regular as clockwork.

Bestius chuckled again. "That's what you get when someone's digging with four arms."

"Four arms?" Gracie asked. "Has he really got four arms?"

"Four arms and not a lot of brain," the dwarf told her. "He's called Clod. The trolls lent him to us to dig out the gold we need—" He stopped and gave a small, awkward cough. "Ahem."

Gracie noticed his discomfort. "Is there a problem, Mr. Dwarf?"

Bestius pulled at his beard. Emboldened by the cover of darkness, he said, "Erm . . . got a bit of a confession."

"A confession? What kind of a confession?" Gracie asked.

Bestius coughed again. "Ahem. Me and the bat— we did a deal. The trolls lent us Clod, but they wanted something in return."

Gracie was remembering something Marlon had said to her earlier in the day. "A princess," she said slowly.

"Marlon said Marcus was going to find a princess, but he never said what for."

"That's right, miss." Bestius took a deep breath. "It was a swap, see—we dug you out, and your young man found us a princess. And I was to take the princess down to King Thab—he's the troll king—but she wasn't going to be there long, because the prince was going to come galloping in and rescue her. But we never did dig you out, did we?"

Bestius waited for Gracie to scream, or faint, or do whatever human girls did when they were badly shocked, but Gracie did none of those things. There was a thoughtful pause before she asked, "What's the princess expected to do, exactly?"

"I've no idea." Bestius's surprise showed in his voice. "The king wants her. I think he's lonely."

"Poor thing," Gracie said sympathetically. "But I don't think any of the princesses from the Five Kingdoms would be very good at talking to a troll."

The dwarf cleared his throat. "The prince said he'd find one somehow. He was desperate to make sure you were safe; gave us his royal word, he did."

"Ah." There was a world of meaning in Gracie's voice. "You know what?" she went on. "I think we should try to get out now." She bent down and shook

Gubble. He woke with a grunt. "Dark," he remarked. "Go home. Cake."

Bestius stood up. "If the Flailing mines are that way, there must be a supply tunnel somewhere very near here. Probably a train track. If I can locate that, we can dig through to it, and then—there you have it! We'll be popping out in the Unreliable Forest in no time at all."

"That sounds wonderful," Gracie said. "Which way do you think Marcus will come with the princess? If he's found one, that is."

"He'll bring her to the diggings in the forest, I'd say." Bestius, much cheered by having made his confession, sounded confident. "He won't know where the troll tunnel is; he needs me to take him there."

Gracie gave a small relieved sigh. "That's OK, then. We might even be in time to meet him." She pulled herself to her feet. "Come on, Gubble. What are you doing?"

Gubble didn't answer at first; then he said, "Shh. Hear things."

Gracie and Bestius froze, listening intently. Gracie's human ears heard nothing, but Bestius gave a sharp whistle. "Yes! Clanking and rattling! The supply train! Mr. Troll, you're a genius. Not too far away, either.

Should be able to dig through from here in thirty minutes max. Hmm. Too many roots where we are just now. Let's go back a few steps, and then I'll start digging. Now, is that a stroke of luck, or a stroke of luck?"

As Gracie and Gubble followed a cheerily whistling Bestius, there was a stirring at the bottom of the deep pit. Oolie's claw-like hand appeared first, followed by her head. Seeing the fallen ladder, she inspected it carefully before smiling a singularly unpleasant smile.

"So dwarfies is here," she muttered, and with a heave she pulled herself out of her secret passageway. Like an evil, overlarge spider, she scrabbled her way up the sides and arrived at the top, where she stopped to catch her breath before making her way into the main tunnel. The heap of earth that had fallen on Mullius distracted her for a moment; she sniffed around it suspiciously. There was still the dank smell of Old Troll in the air, and she scratched herself as she considered what this could mean. "Is the Trueheart caught? Is caught already?"

She turned to peer into the darkness while she felt in her pocket for her tinderbox. Finding it was missing, she growled angrily before bending down and feeling the hard-packed earth floor with her bony fingers. A moment later she was crawling on her hands and knees, mumbling in surprise. "Mullius. Dwarf. Trueheart . . . and what's this? Troll? More troll? What troll? But Mullius this side . . . Trueheart that . . . yes, yes, yes."

Oolie's eyes gleamed. It was clear that Mullius had been there, and Gracie too, but there was no clue to suggest they were together. She hurried farther into the tunnel and crouched down once more. This time she put her ear to the ground and lay very still for more than a minute.

Then she leaped to her feet, panting with excitement. "Yes, yes, yes, yes! Is footsteps! Trueheart footsteps! Is coming to Oolie . . . and Oolie will be ready. Oh, yes. Oolie won't be caught again by sly little Trueheart's tricks. Oolie will have her this time." And the hunched and hideous creature licked her lips before she set off after Gracie.

Chapter Twenty-one

Marcus, guided by Alf, had ridden some ways ahead of the coach and come to a fork in the track. When Alf wheeled to the right, Marcus followed; it didn't occur to him until a few moments later that this was a much narrower path and could easily be missed. He pulled his pony to a halt and considered the situation. It was beginning to get dark, and with nighttime coming it would be all too easy for the coachman to go the wrong way; he also saw, now that he had stopped, a turning circle for the coach not far ahead. "Oh, bother," he said out loud. "What should I do? Do I let them go home? Or what? I can't let them get lost in the forest. After all, it's my fault they're here."

Alf came swinging back. "Is there a problem, Mr. Prince?"

Marcus rubbed at his head to try to clear his thoughts. As he did so he felt a twitching in his jacket pocket and remembered Flo. He looked down and saw her crawling out; a moment later she was in the air flying a woozy circle.

"Hello," he said. "Are you feeling better?"

The little bat dipped in her flight and came to rest on Marcus's sleeve. After a couple of sneezes, she said, "Excuse me—I know I'm only a bat, but Gracie Gillypot shouldn't be in any tunnels." She began to quiver. "There's danger down there for a Trueheart."

"That's what I thought," Marcus agreed. "And I'm on my way; I really am." He rubbed at his head again. "But what about the dwarves? I said I'd get them a princess if they dug Gracie out . . . but it sounds as if they haven't done anything of the kind." This thought made him sit up straighter on his pony. "And if that's the case, I don't need to drag Marigold through the forest to have tea with a troll, do I? So I'll tell her and Vincent to go home." He picked up Glee's reins— then hesitated. "It'd be nice if I could get a message to Gracie—so she knows I'm on the way . . ."

"I'll go," Flo said at once. "I'll tell Gracie Gillypot you're coming." And before Marcus could stop her, she was flitting up into the twilight.

Alf flew after her but was back within seconds, looking peevish. "She says I should stay with you," he reported. "Says I'd slow her down. Me! Uncle Marlon says I'm the speediest—"

"Shh!" Marcus held up his hand. "Can you hear something? Some kind of thumping—OH!" His eyes widened. "Do you know what I think it is? I think it's that troll—the one we saw in the clearing. It's exactly the same *thud-thud-thud* noise. . . . Oops! It's making the path shake!"

Marcus was right. Glee was moving restlessly, his ears flicking to and fro.

Alf put his head on one side. "Quite deep down, I'd say. Don't think he'll pop up under our noses." He sounded regretful.

"I should hope not," Marcus said with feeling. "Come on. Let's send Marigold on her way." He turned the weary Glee around and rode back down the track, Alf flying high above his head.

The coach came into sight sooner than Marcus had expected. The lamps were lit, and the four white horses were trotting steadily along in the twilight.

"Well done," he said as the coachman pulled the horses to a halt. "If you take the right fork ahead, you'll find a place where you can turn."

The coachman nodded. "Flailing road."

Vincent's head popped out of the window. "Marigold wants to know if there are any bats out there. And when are we going to go home?"

"I was just telling Fingle," Marcus explained. "You'll be heading home in no time at all."

Vincent vanished, to be replaced by Marigold. "You were gone *ages*," she complained.

"No, I wasn't," Marcus said indignantly.

Marigold sniffed. "I want you to ride with us until we turn around. I think you're up to something."

Marcus was about to protest, but changed his mind. It wasn't far to the Flailing road, and he still felt a certain responsibility for Marigold. "OK," he said, and he did his best to be patient as the coach lumbered onward.

Ten minutes later it reached the right-hand fork, and there were loud protesting squeals from Marigold as the track grew more and more stony and rutted; Marcus grinned to himself as he heard Vincent shrieking in unison. His grin disappeared, however, as they got nearer the turning circle. Glee kept shying at shadows and dancing sideways, and it was all Marcus could do to keep him from galloping off between the tall and gloomy trees that overhung the narrow pathway.

"Hush, boy," Marcus said soothingly. "Hush. . . . It's OK. We'll be on our way soon." He patted the pony and talked him past the trees and into the open space, but once there, Glee threw up his head and whinnied loudly. The horses pulling the coach caught the note of panic and began to buck in their harness; the coachman pulled them to the side of the clearing, where they calmed down a little, but their eyes were still wild, and there was foam on their bridles.

Vincent and Marigold wrenched open the window. "What's happening?" Vincent gasped. "Is it monsters?"

"Or murderers?" Marigold was clutching at his arm. "Fingle! Save us!"

The coachman didn't answer. He was staring at the center of the clearing, and as he stared the clouds floated away from the slow-rising moon and silver light shone down. The deep scar that split the clearing in two was clear to see and steadily widening. A second crack zigzagged suddenly toward the coach, making Marigold and Vincent scream so loudly that Glee shivered and stamped his feet. Fingle, galvanized into action, leaped off his driving seat and began frantically trying to unbuckle the harness and release the horses.

"Oops!" Alf was on Marcus's shoulder. "That troll sure is causing a commotion!"

Marcus, shocked into silence, merely pointed.

The crack was widening into a chasm, a chasm filled with darkness. Darkness—until an eye appeared, far down, but still clear in the moonlight. It looked puzzled as it gazed wonderingly up. "Yug," rumbled a voice. "Yug."

Marigold slammed the window shut, pulled down the blind, and buried her head under a cushion. Vincent crouched beside her and promised that if he was saved, he'd be good forever and ever and ever and EVER.

And the coach began to lurch toward the chasm.

Chapter Twenty-two

If Queen Bluebell of Wadingburn had seen Professor Scallio's somewhat unorthodox method of traveling, she might have had doubts as to his suitability as tutor to her grandchildren. On the other hand, she was a broad-minded woman and might simply have regarded it as another of his interesting eccentricities. After all, his sister was one of the Ancient Crones, so allowances had to be made.

Once outside the palace, the professor had looked to the left and right to make sure he was unobserved before slipping into a small but extremely dense thicket of exotic shrubs and bushes, grown with much pride by Bluebell's head gardener and strictly out-of-bounds to everyone—including Bluebell herself. After checking carefully that he really was alone, Professor Scallio had taken off his scholar's robe, turned it inside out, and given a sharp series of high-pitched whistles. He had then sat down to wait.

The first bats to fly out of the evening gloom were not known to the professor; he'd thanked them for their swift response and carried on watching to see if Alf or Millie appeared, but there was no sign of them. Gradually more and more bats had come flying into the thicket, until at last there were enough for the professor's purpose. Guessing that Marlon's family must be busy elsewhere, he had decided he could wait no longer and gave his instructions. Hundreds of bats settled themselves on his robe, clinging to the silken cords that covered it; a moment later he was lifted off the ground. Anyone watching from the palace would have seen Prince Vincent and Princess Loobly's tutor apparently walking exceedingly fast; it would have taken very sharp eyes to spot that his fur-covered cloak was made up of a thousand quivering wings and his feet were not touching the path.

Once he was out of sight of the palace windows, the professor's speed increased considerably. He struck out over fields and farmland and, by taking the most direct route to the border of the Five Kingdoms, was there far sooner than Queen Bluebell could ever have imagined.

The bats were puffing hard, and the somewhat portly professor felt a pang of guilt. "Thank you so much, fellows," he said. "Really appreciate it." He peered around, but there was no sign of Vincent or Marigold. Fresh hoof-and-wheel marks made it clear that the coach had been there earlier; it did not require any great powers of investigation to see it had gone up the track that would eventually lead to the Flailing road. There was nothing to suggest it had returned. Professor Scallio raised his eyebrows and considered his options. A silk cushion and a discarded daisy chain suggested that Marigold had reached her destination, but Fedora's pony and cart were missing. It was, therefore, possible that Marigold was even now safely on her way home—but why was Vincent, well known for his remarkable lack of initiative and bravado, heading away from the Five Kingdoms? Could Marigold have persuaded him to help her in her newly discovered desire for adventure? Scallio sighed and began to negotiate with the bats.

It was beginning to look as if he might have a mutiny on his hands when a sharp little voice squeaked, "Oi! What do you think my dad would say if he heard you complaining and moaning and carrying on like that?"

"Oh, Millie!" The professor beamed. "I'm so very glad to see you. I need to follow those tracks and see where they go."

Millie fluttered down, frowning at the mutineers, who were all trying to explain at once that they hadn't meant it, no, not at all, and it would be their great pleasure to carry Miss Millie Batster's friend wherever he wanted to go—even if he was quite exceptionally heavy and they were completely exhausted.

"They've got a point," Professor Scallio said. "Too much sitting around reading makes a chap stout. But if they could give me a lift so I can catch up with Queen Bluebell's royal coach, I'd be profoundly grateful—and I promise I'll make my own way home."

"A coach?" Millie asked. "What coach?" The professor explained his mission to find Vincent and Marigold, and Millie nodded before flying onto his shoulder. "I'm looking for Dad," she said in a hushed whisper. "I think he might have gotten himself into terrible trouble with the Ancient Crones. I'm ever so worried about him."

"Surely not!" the professor said, startled.

"And I'm worried about Miss Gracie as well," Millie went on. "But let's find this coach first." She sighed. "Wouldn't be surprised if Dad was interfering there as well. There's no stopping him at the moment. I'll come with you, and I'll tell you all about it on the way." She gave a few terse orders, and the bats hurried into position. A moment later, Prince Vincent's tutor was traveling once more.

Chapter Twenty-three

Bestius had, after making Gracie and Gubble walk considerably farther than "a few steps" back along the tunnel, finally found what he considered an ideal place to dig a hole through to the dwarves' railway track. From time to time Gracie sent sparks flying from her tinderbox so she could check his progress and was amazed at the speed with which he worked. Already there was a sizable hole, and Bestius hardly seemed tired at all.

"Wouldn't you have thought Marlon would be back by now?" Gracie asked wistfully. "It seems such a long time since we saw him."

"Time does strange things down here." Bestius paused for a moment. "Seems like hours when it's only minutes. Why, I remember one time—" He stopped mid-sentence. "Did you hear something?"

Gracie's pulse began to race. "Like what?"

"A sneeze." Bestius sounded puzzled rather than nervous.

"Flo!" Gracie pulled out her tinderbox, and a joyous flurry of twinkling stars soared into the air. "Flo! We're here! Where are you?"

Flo whizzed into the light, flapping her wings in agitation. "No! No! Put it out, Gracie Gillypot! She's after you . . . I saw her! Run, run as fast as you can!"

"What? Who's coming?" Bestius held his spade in front of him as a weapon.

"It's Oolie!" Gracie gasped and grabbed Gubble's hand. "She's horrible! She caught me before — she's evil — Oh, come ON, Gubble!"

The troll stood his ground. "Urk. Badness. Gracie run. Gubble stay."

"Oolie?" The dwarf began to tremble. "The dwarf catcher?" He dropped his spade and caught Gracie's wrist. "But she's dead — isn't she?"

"No! She's here!" Gracie tugged at Gubble's arm. "She wants to catch me because I'm a Trueheart. *Please,* Gubble! RUN!"

"Gubble stay." The troll gave Gracie a push. "Go!"

Gracie staggered but was saved from falling by Bestius. "Do as he says," he ordered. "If he can hold her off, we can make a dash for that hiding place."

"I can't leave him—" Gracie began, but Bestius pulled her away. As tears filled her eyes, she heard sounds of battle behind her: hissing and grunting and snarling and an ominous series of thumps, followed by a long, high-pitched scream that could have been either triumph or pain.

"There's nothing you could have done," Bestius panted as they ran. "She's a monster! Gubble's our only hope."

Gracie was sick with terror, and her mind was whirling. What had happened to Gubble? Her breath was rasping in her chest, and it was becoming harder and harder to keep moving. She was doing her best not to break down and cry when her feet suddenly slid from under her and she fell heavily, dragging Bestius down with her. "Ow," she wailed. *"Ow."*

"Shh!" The dwarf's voice was urgent, and Gracie stuffed her hand in her mouth. "Shh . . . I can hear her! She's coming! Can you get up?"

"Quick! Quick!" Flo was squeaking above them.

Gracie pulled herself up, every bone in her body protesting as she did so. She took a limping step, and it was then that she realized what she had slipped on. "The oil!" she whispered. "The oil from the lamp." Turning, she pulled the tinderbox from her pocket.

Her hands were trembling so much, it took her three attempts to get it to work, but at last sharp splinters of light flew up — and the oil caught fire.

A wall of flames leaped into the air; for an agonizing moment Gracie thought she was in danger, but the roaring furnace missed her by inches, and it was Oolie who was engulfed. For a millisecond the dwarf catcher was sharply outlined as a twisted silhouette; the next minute she had melted away into a gruesome puddle of greenish slime. The fire crackled angrily around it before gradually sinking into a pool of glowing red embers.

Gracie gulped, tried to swallow her feelings but couldn't, and burst into tears.

As Bestius patted her on the back, a small, familiar shape came hurtling through the air, squeaking in agitation. "Run, kiddo! He's behind me! Run!"

Gracie looked at Marlon and rubbed at her tear-stained cheeks. "I can't," she said miserably. "I just can't run anymore. . . . I'm too tired."

"C'mon, kid!" Marlon exhorted. "You're a Trueheart! Never give up 'n' all that!" He flew an urgent circle close to her head. "You can do it!"

"Can do it!" Flo echoed.

But already an ominous shadow was filling the tunnel.

Bestius gave a low groan, and Gracie knew it was too late. She and the dwarf were trapped . . . and as the massive bulk of Mullius Gowk bore down on her, she stood as straight as she could and waited for the worst.

With a deep rumble of satisfaction, Mullius seized his prey by the hair with the intention of dragging her behind him — but as his fingers touched the silver thread in Gracie's braids, he gave a sharp yelp of pain and abruptly dropped her. With an angry growl he tried again; again he was forced to let her go. Bellowing with pain and frustration, he scooped her up, tucked her under a huge knobbly arm, grabbed Bestius, and then, squeezing them both so hard they gasped for breath, turned to stomp his way back to the royal apartments, where King Thab was eagerly waiting.

Marlon, hidden in the shadows, wiped his eyes with a leathery wing before following. Flo, sniffing loudly, flew behind him.

Ten minutes later the somewhat bumped and bruised but still solid figure of Gubble came limping up to inspect the remains of the glowing embers. He stared at them for some time before remarking, "Ug." Stamping his way across, he continued on up the tunnel, a faint smell of singed troll lingering behind him.

Chapter Twenty-four

Clod's one aim in life was to do as he was told. His brain was too small to cope with any kind of decision; when he looked up and saw a large coach toppling into the crevasse that he had unintentionally created, he had no thought of moving out of the way. Instinct made him hold out his four arms as it began to fall; instinct made him attempt to catch it—but the weight was too much even for his incredible strength, and he was flattened beneath the wheels. For a moment he lay completely still while stars zigzagged around the end of his nose and strange humming noises filled his head.

Marcus, peering down in terror from above, fully expected to see the coach smashed into a thousand pieces. He was astounded to see it apparently unharmed, the top gleaming smooth and unscathed in the moonlight. "Wow!" he breathed.

Fingle came to stand beside him. "Dwarf mine," he remarked. "Or troll tunnel. All over the place around here."

"Oh . . ." Marcus scratched his head while he tried to take in what had happened. At the bottom of the chasm the coach began to rock to and fro, and the sound of wailing floated up.

"Them two inside is all right, then." The coachman was impassive. "I suppose I'll be expected to wait here for the time being, seeing as my coach is down that hole, like." He pulled his cloak closer around his shoulders and folded his ham-like arms.

Marcus stared at him in astonishment. Fingle was as calm as if coaches vanished in front of him every day of the week. "Erm . . . yes," he said. "That is—I don't really know." The wailing grew louder. "I'd better go and see if Marigold and Vincent are hurt." The coachman's long leather whip caught his eye, and he pointed to it. "Would that be strong enough to hold me if I climbed down? Would you be able to hang on to the other end? Or we could tie it around a tree."

Fingle looked affronted. "I'll hold it. Young whippersnapper like you don't weigh nothing. Don't you go getting muddy footprints on the roof of my coach, now. Takes a lot of hard work to get a shine like that."

As he could think of no answer to this, Marcus silently wrapped the end of the whip around his waist and knotted it. Then, supported by Fingle, he rappelled down. It was only as he dropped level with the coach doors that he saw a large troll spread-eagled underneath. Marcus shut his eyes.

When he opened them again, the enormous figure was still there, and he was forced to admit to himself that he wasn't dreaming. Or hallucinating. The troll seemed resigned to his position and in no way threatening, and Marcus took a deep breath. "Erm . . . hang on a moment. Don't move. I don't want to step on you."

He landed close to the troll's head and untied himself. Fingle pulled the long leather whip back up, and Marcus was left face-to-face with Clod. He looked at the troll in disbelief; the troll looked back without even the mildest curiosity.

"Erm . . . well done for saving Marigold and Vincent," Marcus said at last. The troll blinked. Praise was something he wasn't used to. Marcus turned to look at the coach; the wailing from inside had changed to a low-level moaning, but when he knocked sharply on the door, there was a startled silence. "It's me, Marcus," he called. "Open the door!"

"No! We won't!" It was Marigold. "We've locked ourselves in and we're not coming out until we're back in the Five Kingdoms. We're covered in bruises and there's salmon paste all over Vincent's velvet suit and my dress is *ruined*!"

Marcus shrugged. Evidently Marigold and Vincent had survived the fall with no serious injury. As his eyes got used to the dim light, he discovered that Clod's vast body was neatly pinned down by the wheels; his upper pair of arms, shoulders, and head were free. "If you wriggle this way," Marcus told him, "you should be able to get out."

The troll made no attempt to move, and Marcus wondered if he was deaf. "WRIGGLE THIS WAY," he repeated.

The result was immediate. Instructions, especially shouted instructions, Clod understood. He began to wriggle, and the coach lurched dangerously from side to side — to an accompaniment of shrill shrieks — until at last he was free.

He made no attempt to get up, and Marcus looked at him in exasperation. "Aren't you going to try to stand?" he asked, and then, as the troll blinked mind-lessly, "STAND UP!"

Clod did as he was told, and Marcus took an anxious

step back as the monstrous figure loomed over him. "Yug?"

Beginning to appreciate how Clod functioned, Marcus ordered, "Sit down!"

Clod sat, and the ground shook. Further instructions led to his standing up again and stomping to the front of the coach. It took several attempts to get him to pick up the shafts, as orders containing more than four or five words confused him, but once he had grasped the idea, he grinned, showing toothless gums.

Marcus, hardly able to believe his luck, scrambled up onto the coachman's seat. "Walk!" he commanded, and Clod walked, dragging the coach behind him as if it weighed nothing. Marcus punched the air in triumph. An idea was forming in his head; what had Fingle said? Troll tunnels . . . Could this be a troll tunnel? Or was it a dwarf mine? As Clod continued to stomp steadily onward into the darkness, Marcus felt a growing sense of excitement. Surely this must be a troll tunnel. And if it was, surely he could find Gracie.

The small window at the front of the coach, designed to enable passengers to pass instructions to the coachman, snapped open, and Marigold's furious face appeared. "Where are we going?" she demanded.

"It's OK," Marcus told her. "Don't worry. We're going to find Gracie, and then——"

Marigold began to scream. She screamed so loudly that Clod came to a sudden and horrified stop. "I want to go HOME!" she shrieked. "Home, do you hear? HOME!"

"Yug." Clod picked up the shafts and, in a maneuver that resulted in a great deal of damage to the corners of the coach and the walls of the tunnel, turned around. "Yug." And he set off at a steady trot. No shouted commands from Marcus could stop him; he had recognized the one word he knew beyond any shadow of a doubt, and he was going home. Marcus could only hang on as they rattled their way back over the heaps of rocks and stones at the bottom of the chasm. Clod made no allowance for the comfort of coach travelers.

"Speedy for a troll, isn't he?" said a cheery voice, and Marcus saw Alf flit down and land on the coach roof. He was immediately jolted off and had to pretend he'd meant to land on Marcus's shoulder all along.

"Alf," Marcus said urgently, "do you know where we're going? And where we are? This is a troll tunnel, isn't it?"

Alf began to answer, but a particularly large boulder came within inches of tipping the coach right over, and Marcus had to lean perilously far out from his seat in order to bring the vehicle back onto four wheels. The noises from inside made it clear that Marigold had landed heavily on Vincent's lap, together with a sponge cake.

"You'll have to shout," he told Alf. "I can't hear anything—Marigold's got a horribly piercing scream."

"I don't know where we are!" Alf was squeaking as loud as he could. "Shall I go and have a look-see?"

Another boulder meant Marcus could only nod in reply, and the little bat waved a wing and disappeared into darkness.

He was back within a couple of minutes.

"It's a dead end ahead," he reported. "Nowhere to go. Solid rock!"

"We'd better hang on tight, then," Marcus warned. "He'll have to turn around, and he doesn't make any allowances for the coach. We'll be lucky if there are any wheels left by the time we get wherever it is we're going." He took a firm grip on the rail beside him and waited for Clod to make a sudden swerve—but the troll kept thundering onward, his head lowered. Marcus paled. "He's not going to try to go through, is he?"

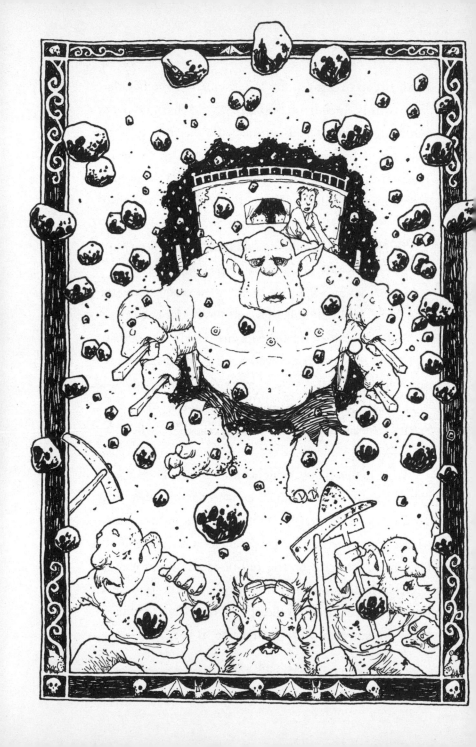

There was no time for Alf to answer. The force with which Clod's head hit the rock jolted every bone in Marcus's body, and he crouched down and put his arms over his head as thick dust swirled around him. The troll took a step back, then launched himself at the rock for a second time. There was a mighty crash and the thunder of falling stones; Clod gave a triumphant grunt and heaved himself and the coach through the gap.

On the other side, dwarves yelled and shrieked and scattered in all directions. Master Amplethumb, balanced precariously on a ladder, was frozen into shocked immobility as the enormous troll appeared, brushing rubble off his shoulders as if he were merely emerging from a snowstorm. Behind him rocked a large traveling coach, and seated on the driving seat was a scruffy young man covered in dust. Master Amplethumb gulped. A moment later the troll was battering his way across to the other side of the mine; there was a second, less thunderous crash — and he and the coach were gone.

Gradually the dwarves began to pick themselves up and view the damage. One by one they relit their fallen lamps, held them high, and studied the heaps of boulders and the wide, jagged opening in the rock. Master

Amplethumb, whose one and only thought was to seize Bestius Bonnyrigg by the neck and hurl him into the deepest dungeon for at least a thousand years, was the last to notice the thick seams of gleaming gold . . . gold, gold, and yet more gold.

Chapter Twenty-five

Gracie's ribs were aching unbearably by the time Mullius reached the candlelit corridor leading to King Thab's royal apartments. Bestius was wheezing badly, and she could see that his face had turned a worrying shade of purple; his eyes were shut tight, and he looked as if he were in acute pain. Ahead of them were huge doors covered in unpleasantly sharp spikes; one was half open, and Gracie had a quick glimpse of a massive room hung with oppressive red velvet drapes. Mullius thrust his way inside, Gracie and Bestius were dropped onto a stone floor covered with animal skins, and the doors were slammed shut. There was the sound of a heavy wooden bar falling into place; Gracie's heart sank, and a cold, clammy hand clutched at her stomach. *Be brave,* she thought. *Think of Marlon. Think of Marcus. They're bound to be looking for you. All you*

need is time for them to get here. Come on, Gracie Gillypot!
Make a plan! She resolutely ignored the question: But
will Marcus know where to look?

"Trueheart," said a gruff voice. "Trueheart . . . Is
you real Trueheart?"

Gracie stood up and looked King Thab in the
eye. She was surprised to see that he was considerably smaller than Mullius, but no hint of this crossed
her face. She took in his mean little eyes and heavy
head, and noticed the weakness of his chin and his
flabby lower lip. He was staring at her greedily, rubbing his hands together; a goblin was crouched on
the back of the throne, and he too was staring at
Gracie. Gracie, very conscious of her mud-stained
clothes and face and her tousled hair, took a deep
breath. *Here goes,* she said to herself, and took a deci-
sive step forward. "My name is Princess Gracie. I
understand you wanted a princess to keep you company. Well, here I am."

King Thab gave an astonished grunt. "Princess?
Not Trueheart?"

Gracie nodded. "That's right. My friend here"—she
turned and pointed at the bruised and bedraggled
Bestius—"my friend here was bringing me to visit you,

so I suggest you thank him and let him go. I understand that was the arrangement?"

Spittle, his eyes gleaming, leaped forward. "May I ask the dwarf — on His Majesty's behalf, of course — if that is true?"

Before Bestius could open his mouth, Gracie said, "I told you. I'm Princess Gracie, and I'm here of my own free will to pay my respects to the king of the trolls."

The king's eyes flicked from Gracie to Bestius and back again. "Princess? Pretty princess?" There was doubt in his voice.

The dwarf struggled to his feet and bowed. "Just as you requested, Your Majesty."

"But . . ." King Thab shook his head as if he were trying to clear a fog from his brain. "But where Trueheart?"

Mullius began to rumble, and Gracie quickly stepped closer to the king. "I think your servant was confused. . . . Was he looking for somebody else?" She did her best to sound affronted. "He was really quite rough when he brought me here, you know. I didn't have any opportunity to explain who I was, or what I was doing. But please don't bother to tell him off — it doesn't matter, because I'm here now. Would you like me to talk to you? I heard you were lonely, and that's why you wanted someone to visit you. Or we could play cards? Do you like playing cards?"

King Thab shook his head again, then gave a half smile. "Yes. Am lonely."

"That's so sad." Gracie leaned forward and patted his rough, scale-covered hand. "Why don't you tell me —" She was interrupted by a growl from Mullius and jumped around to see him staring at the iron box. There was a curious glow surrounding it; with a loud roar, Mullius flung open the lid.

Inside was the heart of glass, now glowing a fierce blood-red; deep in its center beat a steady scarlet pulse. King Thab leaped up and strode toward it, his face alight with excitement.

"Trueheart!" Mullius bellowed, pointing at Gracie. "TRUEHEART!"

"King of Kings!" Thab stretched his arms wide in triumph. "Thab will be King of Kings!"

"NO!" The roar echoed around the cave. "NO!" Mullius Gowk towered over his master. "Mullius! MULLIUS be King of Kings!" With one giant hand, he seized the heart. "End Trueheart's life!" With the other he seized the trembling Gracie by the arm and dragged her toward him. "End Trueheart's life NOW!"

As Gracie twisted and squirmed and beat at him with her fists, he lifted the heart of glass high above his head . . . and a small black bat hurled itself across the cavern, straight into his face. Mullius staggered, and his hand that held the heart sliced down, missing Gracie by a hair's breadth. The Old Troll snarled savagely and caught her by her braids to try again; as the silver thread burned deep into his hand, he gave a shriek of agony and threw her from him.

The heart slipped from his fingers and fell, shattering into a thousand tiny fragments.

For a moment there was a stunned silence . . . until King Thab began to scream in frustrated rage. "No prophecy now! Thab not be King of Kings! No bowing to Thab—never, EVER!" Spittle, Bestius, and Gracie clapped their hands to their ears, but the scream bounced off the walls and went on and on and on. Mullius stood sullenly among the shards of glass, his head drooping . . . and the wooden door splintered into matchwood as Clod came staggering through, still dragging the coach behind him.

King Thab stopped screaming, but the sound continued. Gracie, certain now that she was in the middle of a hideous nightmare, saw a figure that looked like the ghost of Marcus climb stiffly off the snow-white coach.

He shook himself and was enshrouded in a cloud of dust. Then, with a sharp *rat-a-tat-tat,* he knocked on the coach door. "Marigold! Could you please SHUT UP!" Only then did he look around to see where he was, and his eyes and his mouth opened wider and wider until he had the appearance of a startled fish.

"If I were you, kiddo," said a well-known voice, "I'd close your mouth. Moths, remember. Moths."

"MARCUS! I knew you'd come!" Gracie flew across the cavern and flung herself into the prince's arms.

For a second, Marcus's eyebrows rose even higher, but then he grinned happily and enveloped her in a protective bear hug.

"Excuse *me!*" The coach door opened, and Marigold appeared. Her pale blue dress was crumpled and stained, her hair was disheveled, and her face was purple with anger. Completely ignoring Mullius, King Thab, and Spittle, she glared at Marcus. "How DARE you speak to me like that! I've been rattled and jolted and bumped and I'm bruised all over and I think you're completely and utterly horrible, and I'm never, ever, *ever* going to speak to you again because I HATE you! So THERE!" With a stamp of her foot and a toss of her head, she slammed the door shut again so hard that even Clod jumped.

"I guess that means I don't have to walk with her in the wedding procession," Marcus said. He sounded jubilant.

King Thab, who had sunk onto his throne in despair, looked up. "Who that?" he asked, pointing at the coach.

"That," Marcus told him, "is Princess Marigold of Dreghorn. How do you do, by the way? I'm Prince Marcus from the kingdom of Gorebreath." He bowed as politely as if they had been introduced in Queen Bluebell's reception room and held out his hand.

King Thab stared at him, disbelief written all over his face. "You? You prince? And cross-face girl is princess?"

Marcus bowed again.

King Thab turned to Spittle. "Write!" he instructed urgently. "Write! Tell dwarves. No princess for troll. NEVER!"

Spittle did as he was told.

King Thab grunted approval, then considered for a moment, frowning heavily. Mullius stirred, and the king glowered at him. "Banished," he pronounced. "Go. Go FOREVER!" He raised an imperious hand. "Clod! Take Gowk to caves. Deep, deep down. Take Gowk NOW!"

Even if he had tried to protest, Mullius Gowk would have been no match for Clod and his four arms. As it was he went meekly, rumbling deep inside but making no attempt to resist. Clod stomped steadily behind him.

"What'll happen to him?" Marcus asked, but the king simply shrugged.

"Gone," he said. "Gone. Gone like heart of glass. All gone." He put his head in his hands and began to sigh.

Gracie looked at the scattered fragments of glass and then at the dejected figure of the king. The goblin was leaning on the arm of the throne, and she moved nearer. "Isn't there anything we can do?" she said. "He seems so lonely. . . ."

It was Bestius who answered. The disappearance of Mullius and Clod had cheered him immensely, and he was beginning to think he might have a future as Master Amplethumb's assistant after all. "The goblin said something about trouble with a lady . . ."

"Is that true?" Gracie asked.

Spittle nodded. "The king had a wife," he said in a low voice. "Queen Thulka. She wasn't bad, but she asked too many questions, and Mullius marched her home to her mother."

"Then you should go and ask her to come back," Gracie told him. "After all, Mullius isn't here anymore. King Thab and Queen Thulka . . . sounds like a good combination to me."

Thab raised his head and stared at Gracie. "Thulka?"

"You'd like to see her again, wouldn't you?" Gracie spoke to the troll king as gently as if he were a troubled child. "And do you know what? Being a King of Kings wouldn't be that special. People bow to *good* kings, not horrible, scary ones."

A slow smile spread across King Thab's face. "GOOD king," he said. "GOOD!"

The goblin hesitated, then shook Gracie's hand. "Thank you, Trueheart. I'll bring Thulka back as soon as I can."

"Hang on a minute." Bestius fished in his pocket and brought out the gold necklace he had offered the king at the beginning of the day. He laid it on the stone table near Thab's knee. "For your lady wife," he said. "With the compliments of the dwarves."

"Well done, kiddo!" Marlon flew in a celebratory circle around the king's apartments. "Trueheart effect and all that stuff. Gets 'em every time."

Flo, hanging from a roof beam, sighed approvingly.

Marcus grinned at Gracie. "Clever old thing, aren't you?" Gracie smiled back at him, and the coach window opened with a bang.

"Excuse *me*! When EXACTLY are you thinking of taking us home? And don't you even *dream* of telling us we have to walk. We're going to stay in this coach, aren't we, Vincent darling? So you'll just have to find someone or something to pull it."

There was a muffled agreement from inside, and Marcus looked at Gracie and Bestius in perplexity. "Whatever can we do?" he asked.

"Ug," said a voice from the doorway. "Ug."

Chapter Twenty-six

It was late the following morning before Gubble finally hauled the coach containing Marigold and Vincent up onto the Flailing road, while Marcus and Gracie scrambled alongside. They had spent an uncomfortable night dozing in the coach outside King Thab's royal apartments; Marigold and Vincent had made a fuss about sharing space with a troll and a dwarf, and eventually Gubble and Bestius had settled themselves underneath the coach wrapped up in an old horse blanket. They had had by far the most peaceful night, for Marigold had seen Marlon, Alf, and Flo having a merry reunion party by candlelight and, convinced that the bats were about to take up residence in her corner of the coach, had twitched and squealed at every tiny sound. It was a weary party that set out to follow Alf as he led the way back down the windings of the troll tunnel and through the dwarves' shattered gold mine to the sunlit ravine where Clod had changed the landscape forever.

Marcus had expected that they would be forced to abandon the coach at this point, but Master Amplethumb, giddy with delight at the rich new seams of gold that had been revealed, insisted on organizing a team of sturdy dwarves to heave the coach up the fallen rocks to the grassy plateau above. "Least I can do for you, Your Highness," he said. "Thanks to you, we'll be on time with all the orders — so no reason for you to worry about the royal wedding. All the crowns'll be there, and if you should ever be wanting a couple for you and your young lady friend, just you let me know. It'll be no trouble, no trouble at all."

Marcus, who had never had any intention of worrying about the wedding, thanked the dwarf as politely as he could. As the coach bumped and rattled upward, he gave Gracie a sideways look to see if she had heard Master Amplethumb's remarks about lady friends — but she was gazing up at a small bat flying circles above.

"Isn't that Millie?" she asked. "I'm sure it is. Millie! Millie! Is that you?"

Millie came down in one smooth swoop and greeted Gracie with enthusiasm. "Oh! Miss Gracie! I'm so pleased to see you, you can't imagine! Are you all right? I've been thinking of all the dreadful things that could have happened to you, and I've been *so* worried! So's Miss Edna—and it's all Dad's fault!" The little bat paused and frowned. "He's gone too far this time, you mark my words. I never thought you'd hear me say this, but I'm ashamed of what he's been up to; I really am."

"But Millie!" Gracie stared at the bat in astonishment. "Haven't you heard? It was Marlon who saved me! He was *so* brave. He flew at the Old Troll and made him drop the heart of glass! If he hadn't been there, I'd have been killed!"

"What?" Millie's eyes brightened. "My dad did that?"

Gracie nodded. "He was wonderful. Marcus is going to see about getting him a medal. Aren't you, Marcus?"

"Absolutely." Marcus was so emphatic that Millie's last doubts faded away.

"Ooooh," she breathed. "A medal for Dad. Just wait until I tell Alf."

"Alf was there," Gracie told her. "He saw it all. Him and Flo—they were there all the time, up on the roof beams. He'll tell you how brave your dad was."

Millie wiped away a tear. "You've made me very happy, Miss Gracie. I didn't like thinking badly of my dad. Just a minute. . . . Who's Flo?"

Gracie laughed. "She saved me as well. You bats—you're all amazing. I don't know what we'd do without you!"

"I don't think *I* did much," Millie said doubtfully. "Only sorted out Professor Scallio when he was bat-walking. Did you know he's waiting for you at the top of the cliff? Him and a great big coachman?"

Marcus gave a delighted cheer. "The prof? Oh, that's grand. Come on, Gracie—let's go and say hello!"

Much to Millie's pleasure, he took Gracie's hand, and the two of them clambered up to the top of the ravine.

Millie, dizzy with excitement and relief, flew downward to find Marlon. He was sleeping off the excitement of the night in the mine, but was happy to be woken by his ecstatic daughter.

"Wotcher, kiddo," he said fondly. "Thought you weren't speaking to me."

"Dad!" Millie squeaked. "You're a HERO! Miss Gracie told me!"

Marlon blinked and waved a wing. "Never let it be said that Marlon Batster failed in his duty."

*   *   *

When at last the coach reached the grassy plateau, the dwarves waved a hasty good-bye as Master Amplethumb prodded them back to work.

Only Bestius Bonnyrigg remained, his eyes fixed on Gracie. "Good-bye, miss," he said gruffly. "Just wanted to say, you're a fine companion in an emergency. You could be a dwarf, you could."

Gracie flung her arms around him and gave him a hug. "I'll miss you," she said. "But maybe we'll meet again. I do hope so."

Bestius, scarlet with emotion, nodded speechlessly. There was a loud bellow from the bottom of the ravine, and he jumped. "Got to go."

"Just a minute." Gracie pulled at her braid and tweaked out the silver thread. "Here — please take this. You've been so kind, and it'll remind you of me. And I think it's sort of magic."

The dwarf took the thread and studied it with a professional eye. "Much too heavy to be pure silver," he said, and then he whistled. "It's not . . . it's not from the web of power, is it?"

"Gubble gave it to me," Gracie told him. "I don't know where he found it."

Bestius put the thread carefully in his pocket and gave a formal bow. "I'll treasure it. And if ever you should need a helping hand, Miss Gillypot, just ask. Bestius Bonnyrigg is yours to command."

Gracie smiled her full-beam smile. "Thank you so much," she said, and Bestius gave her one last wave before hastily scrambling down to the impatiently waiting Master Amplethumb.

On the far side of the plateau, Professor Scallio and Fingle were deeply engrossed in a game of poker. Fingle had spent the night placidly waiting; the professor had been more anxious — until the coachman had produced a well-thumbed pack of cards. Now they were interrupted by a triumphant shout from Marcus and looked up to see the coach rolling toward them, with Gubble between the shafts. The professor leaped to his feet with a cry of delight; Fingle picked up the cards scattered over the grass.

Vincent was somewhat taken aback to see his tutor waiting for him, but Marigold took it as no more than her due. She insisted that Professor Scallio come sit beside her in the coach and proceeded to recite her exceptionally long list of grievances. The tutor listened patiently but from time to time was obliged to hide a chuckle of amusement with a cough.

Fingle, after a decidedly tight-lipped inspection of

the battered coach, released Gubble and harnessed the four white horses. At the same time, Marcus saddled Glee, and Gracie stood stroking the pony's nose. "Will you be riding back with Marigold and Vincent?" she asked, trying to sound bright and cheerful and as if this was exactly what she was hoping Marcus had in mind. "Haven't you got a wedding rehearsal today?"

"Oh." Marcus looked bleak. "Oh. Yes. I suppose I have."

Professor Scallio, having politely but firmly stopped Marigold midway through her third repetition of the horrors of the previous night, appeared beside him. "I'd say you deserve a day off, young man," he said. "I'll go back with my young friends here and"—a twinkle appeared in his eye—"I'll make certain that your father knows how you saved Princess Marigold and Prince Vincent from the trolls."

"*Saved* us?" Marigold burst out of the coach in fury. "SAVED us? It was all his fault we were there in the first place!"

The professor gave her a thoughtful look. "So did Marcus ask you to wear your sister's wedding dress and drive to the edge of the Five Kingdoms?"

His tone was one of polite inquiry, but Marigold blushed a deep and unattractive plum color. "No," she said grumpily. "No, he didn't. But he did ask me to go on an adventure."

"And now you're safely back," Professor Scallio said smoothly. "Something to tell your sisters about, I'd imagine. Very few princesses have ever had an experience such as yours."

This was an aspect of adventuring that Marigold hadn't thought of. She was silent for a moment, then said, "Yes. Well. I was rather brave, wasn't I?"

"You screamed a lot," Marcus pointed out unhelpfully.

"That," the professor said, "is only to be expected in a young person of Princess Marigold's extreme sensitivity, and something you will never mention again." He gave Marcus a warning glare.

Marigold hesitated. "OK," she said at last. "I give in. Marcus rescued me and Vincent. But I was very, very, *very* brave."

Marcus swept her a deep bow. "The bravest princess there."

The professor hastily opened the coach door. "Time to return you to your mother, Princess. She has been most concerned for your welfare." He turned back to Marcus. "I'll tell your father you're seeing Gracie safely home and you'll be back later, or even tomorrow."

"What about the rehearsal —" Marigold began, but Vincent took her arm.

"Wouldn't it be much nicer to go home on our own, darling?"

Marigold bit her lip and looked angrily at Marcus and Gracie. At last she shrugged. "All right. We can practice walking together without him interfering, and if he's not there, Fedora will see how unreliable he is." She climbed into the coach, and Vincent followed her, shutting the door firmly behind him.

Professor Scallio beamed at Marcus and Gracie and swung himself up beside Fingle. "My regards to the crones," he told them. "Tell that sister of mine I'll be seeing her soon."

"Strange, that, kiddo," Marlon remarked as he flew in a circle around Gracie and Marcus, closely followed by Millie, Alf, and Flo. He waved a wing at Gracie. "Trueheart effect. Works like magic — except on princesses."

Gracie smiled, then put up her hand to cover a yawn. "Sorry," she apologized. "I'm really tired."

"Arf." Gubble, who had been dozing on the roadside, woke with a start. "Arf. Cake?"

"Good thinking." Marcus brightened. "Let's go and

see if there's any left." He turned to Gracie. "You ride Glee, and I'll walk with Gubble." He helped her into the saddle.

As they began to walk away, the ever-observant Alf noticed that Marcus's hand was resting on top of Gracie's. "Wheee!" he squeaked. "Two-by-two stuff—"

"Shh!" Millie cannoned into him and rolled him over in midair. "Don't you say another word, or I'll tell Dad that you kissed Flo!"

Alf stared at her in astonishment, while Flo twittered in embarrassment. "How did you know?"

"I didn't. It was a lucky guess!" And Millie chortled as she whizzed out of her cousin's reach.

Gracie, hearing the squeaking but unaware of the cause, turned around. "Flo!" she called. "Flo! Are you coming with us? Aunt Edna'll cure your hay fever in no time."

Delighted by the invitation, Flo recovered herself sufficiently to zigzag her way onto Gracie's shoulder. "Thank you ever so much," she said. "But do you know what, Miss Gracie? I haven't sneezed once since we had that party last night."

"Maybe it was the tunnels that made you sneeze," Gracie suggested. "But you're still very welcome to come with me."

Flo dithered and looked coy. "Actually," she whispered into Gracie's ear, "I might just stay with Alf, if you don't mind." She stroked Gracie's cheek before circling up to join Alf and Millie, and Gracie watched her go with a fond look.

"Hurrah!" Alf did a victory roll. "We'll give you a guard of honor all the way back home, Miss Gracie! Me and Millie and Flo and Unc . . . Unc? Uncle Marlon—where are you?"

Marlon, perched in between Glee's ears, sighed. "He's a good kid at heart. But noisy . . . very noisy."

Chapter Twenty-seven

In the House of the Ancient Crones, Edna inspected the shimmering silver web with a snort of satisfaction. "No trouble there," she announced. "I expect Gubble and Gracie and Marcus will be back soon."

The trainee crone sitting beside her hiccuped, and Edna looked at her suspiciously. "Are those cake crumbs on your dress? Chocolate cake crumbs?"

Foyce looked guilty. "They might be."

"Hmph." The Ancient One gave her a considering look. "We've still got a way to go with you, Foyce, but at least you're admitting when you've done something wrong. Now, leave what you're doing and go and find Val and Edna. I want a fresh chocolate cake made as soon as possible, and a large pot of tea." She squinted at the sun outside. "You've just about got time."

Sure enough, by the time Marlon came flitting in through the window to announce Marcus, Gracie, and Gubble's arrival, the smell of baking was heavy in the air. Gubble headed straight for the cake plate with a determined expression on his face; it took all Gracie's powers of persuasion to get him to agree to being washed first, and then having his bruises treated.

The Ancient One sat back in her chair and inspected Marcus. There was stone dust in his hair, and the royal tailor would never have recognized his clothes under the layers of dirt, but something about him must have been satisfactory, because Edna was smiling. "Enjoyed yourself?" she inquired.

Marcus scratched his head. "Kind of. Gracie was heroic. She nearly got herself killed, but she hasn't said a word about it."

"She's a Trueheart," Edna said, and sighed. "Not always an easy life. It's good that she's got you as a friend."

"Is it?" Marcus asked, surprised.

"You make a good team," Edna told him. "You're loyal and truthful, and you're very fond of each other."

A slow blush crept up Marcus's neck, over his face, and into his dusty hair. "I'd do *anything* for Gracie," he said fiercely.

"Good," said the Ancient One. "Maybe you should tell her sometime. Now, go and have your tea. That cake smells as if it ought to be taken out of the oven right this minute."

Chapter Twenty-eight

It was difficult for Marigold to tell her story. When she and Vincent finally reached Dreghorn, her mother burst into tears as soon as she saw the battered coach. The queen continued to weep copiously all through Vincent's disjointed and rambling explanations, and she refused to believe that her daughter had been returned to her safe and unharmed. "Oh my poor darling girl whatever have they done to you when Fedora's pretty pony came trotting up the drive—and I will *not* tell you what Fedora said on that subject as no daughter of mine should ever have spoken in such a way or used such terms of abuse—I just knew you were lost to me lost lost lost and gone forever and ever and ever—and with the wedding so near and everything all but organized and what was I to do . . ."

Hortense and Queen Bluebell bore with her as long as they could, but in the end a glass of icy water was called for, and Queen Kesta, water dripping from the end of her nose, finally came to her senses. Even then she was unable to ask any coherent questions, as Fedora seized the moment to list her own complaints and to inform Marigold that she was most certainly *not* going to take any part in the wedding, and if she thought she was going to be a bridesmaid, she was very VERY much mistaken.

This tirade set Queen Kesta off again, and Bluebell took Fedora by the elbow and marched her away to hear a few home truths. She then did the same with Marigold, with the result that the sisters, both extremely red-eyed and apologetic, kissed their mother and each other and made up.

"So now," Hortense said hopefully, "we can all look forward to a wonderful wedding."

Chapter Twenty-nine

THE DREGHORN GAZETTE

We are thrilled and delighted to report that the long-awaited nuptials between Princess Fedora of Dreghorn and Prince Tertius of Niven's Knowe have taken place in the truly splendid setting of Dreghorn Cathedral. The bride looked radiant in a pink satin dress decorated with tiny blue rosebuds, and the groom was resplendent in the red, purple, and gold uniform of the Niven's Knowe Cavalry. Their crowns were of an exceptionally high quality, a fact commented on by many. All the bridesmaids were, of course, exemplars of beauty, modesty, and elegance. Princess Marigold, sister of the bride, surprised us all with her spontaneous rendition of a song, which, we learned later, she had composed herself.

The entire congregation was in complete agreement that they had never heard anything like it; her companion, Prince Vincent, told me, "She's amazing. Really amazing. Amazing. Don't you think so?"

The procession to and from the cathedral was graced by a number of royal personages, including Princes Arioso and Marcus of Gorebreath. Prince Arioso was especially noticeable for the splendor of his attire. Prince Marcus, if we may so remark without incurring the ire of his royal parents, had the appearance of having dressed in something of a hurry. He was seen afterward at the reception in the company of Her Royal Highness Queen Bluebell the Twenty-eighth of Wadingburn, Miss Gracie Gillypot, and a troll. The latter caused some consternation among the more sensitive of our royal personages and was politely requested to leave. I am happy to report that he did so without complaint. He was accompanied by Prince Marcus and Miss Gillypot, and the reception continued without incident. We wish the royal couple every happiness, and hope they will live Happily Ever After.

Marcus, reading the *Gazette* over his brother's shoulder, snorted. "What a load of rubbish!"

Arioso shook his head. "Give the poor reporter a chance. He could hardly say that Marigold's singing was dreadful and Fedora was livid."

"I didn't mean that," Marcus said. "I meant that stuff about beautiful bridesmaids. Gracie's far prettier than the whole lot of them put together."

Arry looked at his twin in astonishment. "I didn't think you noticed things like that."

Marcus blushed and picked up his hat. "I don't. But she is. And I'm just off to see her. We're going to look for dragons. See you later, bro."

When a pair of evil twins threatens the Five Kingdoms with Total Oblivion, Gracie Gillypot and her intrepid friends must save the day.

The Flight of Dragons
The Fourth Tale from the Five Kingdoms

Vivian French

Dragons?" Professor Scallio peered over the top of his spectacles. "MORE dragons? Where were they this time?"

The very young bat perched on a shelf in the ancient library of Wadingburn Palace opened his mouth, but no sound came out. A much older bat, balanced

an excerpt from *The Flight of Dragons*

precariously on a pile of books on the professor's desk, gave him a sharp look. "Give us the gossip, kiddo. Quick smart! No time to hang about!"

The very young bat began to quiver. "If you please, Mr. Marlon Batster," he whispered. "I ain't accustomed to human people."

Marlon gave a snort of disapproval. "Thought you wanted to learn the biz."

"Oh, I do, Mr. Marlon Batster! I do!" The little bat flapped his wings. "When you said I could be a Batster Super Spotter, I was so excited, I was all of a flap, so to speak, but I didn't know you'd want me to talk to human people." He gave the professor a nervous glance. "They're SCARY!"

"Not as scary as I'll be if you don't spill the beans, young Samson," Marlon said cheerfully. "Come on, kid. You can do it. How many dragons? Where? What time?"

Samson screwed up his eyes and took a deep breath. "Three of them. One gold, one blue, and one green. Beyond the southern border. Twilight yesterday."

"That's more like it," Marlon told him. "Now hop to. You know the drill. Any more sightings and you're back here, pronto."

"Yes, Mr. Marlon Batster, sir. Certainly, Mr. Batster, sir. Erm . . . Mr. Batster?"

⇜ an excerpt from *The Flight of Dragons* ⇝

Marlon lifted an imperious claw. "Spit it out, kid."

"Ma said I had to go straight back to bed, Mr. Marlon Batster, sir."

Marlon sighed. "Can't get quality help these days. OK, young Samson. Scoot." Samson scooted, and Marlon turned to Professor Scallio. "So. What d'you make of that?"

The professor shook his head and picked up a piece of paper from his desk. "That's the fourth time your spotters have seen dragons in the South. There's one report from the North, two from the West, and so far nothing definite from this side of the Five Kingdoms, although Millie heard a farm boy telling his friends he'd seen a dragon. Luckily he'd spent most of the afternoon in the Pig Catcher's Tavern, so nobody believed him."

"Good girl, my Millie." Marlon allowed himself a fond smile. "Not much gets past her."

Professor Scallio stroked his chin. "So far the dragons have been seen only at daybreak and twilight, and they're flying well outside the borders and keeping away from humans. But there's something going on . . . and it's worrisome. Very worrisome. What could they want?"

Before Marlon could answer, the library door flew open. Prince Marcus, second in line to the throne of

*an excerpt from *The Flight of Dragons**

Gorebreath, came striding in, his hair standing on end and his riding jacket covered in mud. "Hi, Prof!" he said. "Nina-Rose is staying at our place, and I can't stand it any longer, so I came to see you. Arry's behaving like a dying duck in a thunderstorm, and Father keeps talking about 'jolly little lovebirds, ho-ho-ho!' and Mother's flapping around like a headless chicken. It's murder. I was going to go and see Gracie, but Mother wants me at home tonight for a hideous family dinner, so I'm going tomorrow instead. It's Gracie's birthday soon, by the way. Thought I'd take her on an adventure—but I don't know where yet. Oh! Hello, Marlon! Didn't see you there!"

"Hi, kiddo."

Marlon didn't sound his usual chirpy self, and Marcus swung around to inspect him. "What's up? You and the prof plotting something?"

The professor and the bat exchanged self-conscious glances, and Marcus brightened visibly. "You *are*! What is it?" He looked at the pile of books on the desk, and his eyes grew wide. "*Dragons: An Introduction. The Larger Beasts of the Five Kingdoms—with pencil illustrations. Illnesses, Abscesses, and Heat Complaints with Reference to Dragons and Other Scaled Beasts*. Wow! Have you found one? A dragon?"

⤏ an excerpt from *The Flight of Dragons* ⤎

"Certainly not." Professor Scallio folded his arms. "Nothing of the kind. I . . . I was just doing some research. On dragons. Wasn't I, Marlon?"

"Sure thing, Prof. Research 'n' all that stuff," Marlon agreed.

Marcus had opened one of the books and was flicking through the pages. "Hey," he said, "look at this! It's Niven's Knowe — there's a drawing of a whole load of dragons outside Terty's palace! How come?"

A pained expression crossed the professor's face. "A flight of dragons, dear boy. A flight."

"A what?" Marcus looked blank.

His old tutor clicked his tongue disapprovingly. "Really, Marcus. Didn't I teach you anything? Collective noun. Herd of cows. Flock of geese. Flight of dragons."

⊿ an excerpt from *The Flight of Dragons* ⊾

Welcome to the Five Kingdoms!

Land of talking bats, vengeful witches, troublesome trolls, silly royal families, numerous evils, and one very good and brave girl named Gracie Gillypot.

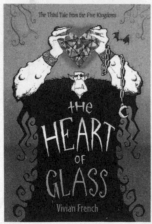

www.candlewick.com